STRANGE TALES

OF THE

WEST

STRANGE TALES

OF THE

WEST

by James "Doc" Manniken

Wire Road Press

Rogers, Arkansas

2014

ISBN-13: 978-0-9909657-0-1
ISBN-10: 0990965708

Cover artwork, photo and layout by noir33.com

Wire Road Press
820 South Fourth Street
Rogers, Arkansas 72756

To my parents,

James and JoAnn Miller

Contents

Strange Tales of the West

The Other

i.

As Fell rode leadenly through the arid canyon, its walls rising on every side like a grave, the weird was on him again. The wind was whispering, sibilant words he could almost make out, though he didn't want to, and every heap of stones seemed a makeshift grave, every rounded rock a skull. The sun beat down, and he sat slumped in the saddle, weary and aching. His horse trudged along the dry waterbed, head low, as if, like him, prey to her own thoughts. The clatter of her hooves, ringing back from the rock, re-echoed through his mind, stirring images that were not quite memories. The experience was not a pleasant one, and he shifted a bit, trying to shake it off.

Coming around a bend, he saw the bodies. His first thought was Indians, and he pulled the rifle from its scabbard, reining up and scanning quickly in every direction. But the canyon was as still as death and there wasn't a sound, just the sighing of the wind; far off a crow cawed. He sniffed the air: nothing but dust, and baking rock. He was alone with the dead.

He replaced the rifle and dismounted, right hand on his pistol-butt, and walked forward as quietly as a ghost. There were two bodies, a man and a pack-horse. No arrows. The horse lay in the litter of its baggage: picks, shovels, saddlebags, pans, a bedroll. There was white around its mouth, and the ribs showed beneath the skin. The man lay a little ahead, the reins still in his hand. He might have been sixty or more, with a heavy grey beard and long straggly hair, and his worn and patched clothes showed he hadn't been too prosperous. Fell was about to turn away when one of the old man's eyes opened.

"Goddamn," Fell breathed and knelt beside him. "Hey there, old timer," he said gently. "Where are you hurt?"

There was pain and sadness in the old man's face. His lips moved but nothing came out. He tried again: "Gut shot." The words came out in a gasp. "They gut shot me... Left me to die."

Fell saw now the blackish stain at the man's midsection. The blood had pooled on the ground, soaking into the sand and dust. There wasn't much he could do.

"Water," the old man whispered. Fell went to the horse and picked up the canteen, military issue, like his. Crouching down again, he raised the old man's head and held the canteen to his lips. The old man drank a little and choked, and a shudder went through him. He wasn't going to last much longer.

"Who done this to you, mister?" Fell said.

"Young fellers," the old man said. "Robbed me. Took my mule. She was loaded heavy. I finally hit it. Always knew I would... Sorry bastards."

"What did they look like?" Fell said.

"Jumped me... Shot my horse and laughed. She looked right at me as she died..."

"What did they look like?" Fell asked again. His flesh was crawling; the weird was very strong.

"Young fellers," the old man whispered. "One had... red hair... no beard. T'other two... looked just alike. Might have been... twins. Mean sons of bitches."

He coughed again. Fell could see how much it hurt him. The cough went on, the old man wheezing for breath; red foam came to his lips. He died.

Fell stood up. The canyon reeled about him like a drunken tomb. Red hair...

How many times had it all replayed itself in his mind? He wanted to forget. He'd been the one who'd taken a liking to the kid in the first place. Or maybe he'd just felt sorry for the boy's mother, with her drunkard husband and half-retarded child. But for all his manifest stupidity, the kid was cunning, and crafty. He killed Max, for their money –Max, Fell's last friend from the Corps, who'd saved his life at Nashville. Fell swore vengeance over Max's grave –swore his life to it –but the little bastard got away.

Staring vacantly at the corpse, no longer seeing it, did he remember, or try not to remember? It was all the same; there was no longer any difference. They'd camped outside of

Fort Smith, near the Arkansas River, and Fell had wanted to go into town. There'd been a girl there once, in one of the dancehalls. Max thought about coming along but he was tired and his old wounds were hurting, and that was when the kid suggested a game. Max loved to play cards, and so Fell rode into town alone. But the dancehall was burned to the ground and of course the girl was gone, and Fell just turned around, thinking how the past was past and you can't go back again, 'cause there aren't any second chances. When he rode back into camp the fire was burning low and the first thing he noticed was the kid's horse was gone. That seemed strange. Then he found Max lying on his side and holding his stomach, and he knew his friend was dying.

"I won all his money," Max said, and spit out blood. "He got mad, called me a cheat... Pulled on me and shot me. I wasn't even wearing my gun. I'm sorry, Fell, he took our stake, too."

That had to have been the kid's plan all along; the game was just an excuse. The stake was almost five hundred dollars in twenty-dollar coins. They'd planned to start over in California.

Max wouldn't be starting over. He was tough: he lasted till dawn, dying as the sun came up. Fell buried him there, on the east bank of the Arkansas, and started after Sanford.

Fell sighed. Oh, the kid was cagey, alright! He'd slipped through Fell's fingers, till that night in the plains of Indian Territory...

But he was close, now. He *knew* it. The kid was probably in some mining town nearby, spending the old man's gold. The little bastard had always gone for easy money. Fell hoped so; he'd enjoy killing him all the more. But it didn't really matter. The kid could have gotten religion and be preaching the Gospel, for all Fell cared. He'd kill him anyway. Finding and killing that son of a bitch was the only thing that gave his life meaning. After that, he didn't care what happened. It didn't matter; nothing did. His soul was already poisoned anyway.

The canyon floor was too rocky to dig a grave, so he covered the old prospector's body with stones. He was standing next to it when the Other slid back down inside his skin; and he knew it had taken the old man's soul. The knowledge sickened him and he turned away, fists clenched, but there was no helping it.

The horse he had to leave where it was, but he knew the vultures and coyotes would take care of it. He went carefully through the old man's packs and saddlebags, hoping to find papers or a letter, anything so he might notify his kin. But there was nothing. The man must have come west before the War and spent the rest of his life prospecting. And here when he'd finally made a strike, some damned fools had gunned him down for it. Once his body was gone he'd disappear from the earth as completely as if he'd never been. But wasn't that true for every man?

The afternoon was almost gone. Fell mounted up, his heart black. The scene burned itself into his mind: the heap of dry stones covering the old man's body; his wretched possessions, scattered like so much trash; the old horse he'd loved, and mourned when it died, now a carcass beginning to swell in the heat. This had to be the kid's work: one more crime to pay in Hell. Fell was going to be glad to help him along with that.

He rode on. By sundown, he figured he'd spotted the town.

ii.

It was a mining town, thrown up helter-skelter on a flat enough spot in a range of saw-back ridges. Above and below, in every direction, you could see claims and men working them. A tinkle of piano music drifted on the wind and Fell smelled food cooking. He pulled up and sat his horse, looking at it. There was a main street that crawled along the ridge and one cross street, hardly long enough to merit the name. Fell could make out a general store, several saloons, a hotel, and the Wells Fargo office. He wondered if the place had a marshal. He doubted it. The town didn't look like it had been there very long. That made it all the more likely the kid was there: he shied clear of the law.

Fell dismounted and sat down on an outcropping of rock, still wracked by memory. Gazing emptily at this broken, sun-baked land, he saw again the debacle at Nashville. He'd have been dead if it hadn't been for Max... Their patrol was screening the southwest side of the city, west of the redoubts that covered the Confederate left flank. The fifteenth of December dawned cold and overcast, the horses stamping and shivering as steam poured from their nostrils. By seven-thirty freezing rain was falling, the ice covering everything. You couldn't see two hundred yards. The men's chins were in their coats as they rode, trying vainly to keep their carbines dry enough to fire. No one even suspected that the Yanks were massing for an assault; it was unimaginable! When at noon the cannons began to roar, you couldn't feature why. "Damn Yankees," Max said. "They got cannon-shot to burn." It was just like everything else. Then, like ghosts coming out of the falling ice, three cavalry divisions hit them.

Fell's mouth went dry at the memory. His men had almost no time to react before the attack was upon them. At first it was slaughter, though the boys died bravely. One of the young ones –what had been his name? –grabbed up the fallen standard and the men rallied briefly on the road; but the Yanks were just too many, and pushed them back. They tried to stand at the railroad line, and failed; and all afternoon they gave ground as the fight took its toll, man after man shot from the saddle, to choke out his life on the frozen ground. Only nightfall spared the survivors, and darkness found them on the far Confederate left, bloodied and depleted, now badly outnumbered.

The night was bitterly cold. At dawn, half-frozen and grim-faced, they waited for the attack as the enemy regrouped before them, less than half a mile away. Picks and shovels bounced off the frozen ground, and at length they gave it up as useless. You could smell bacon cooking over the Yanks' campfires. Fell saw tears in some of the boys' eyes but the wretched scarecrows never uttered a word of complaint. They waited all day, like beasts for slaughter, till finally the Federal attack began, just after three-thirty. There was maybe an hour and a half of daylight left.

The heavy column came on like a blue tide, inexorable. Fell's company hit them head-on, but rolled back under the assault. To their right, deafening, Union batteries pounded the entrenchments on the hill. Fell's company reformed and the men threw themselves in the teeth of the oncoming bluecoats. It was hopeless, and he was sure he would die there –but the order came to disengage. As the enemy threw its weight against the Confederate left, Fell's men pulled back to the Granny White Pike, determined to hold an escape route open, come what may. As they reached their position, it was getting dark. They dismounted and threw a barricade of rails and brush across the pike. The ground was covered with snow, and the drizzling rain froze on top, leaving it slippery as glass. Just at dark, flushed with success, the Federal cavalry bore down upon them in a headlong charge. Men and horses could scarcely keep their footing and all you could see was the flash of musket and pistol fire. The horses reared and plunged, the troopers slashing and thrusting; all about were shouts, and cries of pain, the clang of sabres, the rattle of gunfire. Fell's fingers were so numb with cold, he could hardly cock his pistol. As his men countercharged, a Yankee captain lunged at him. They grappled blindly. Fell fired and missed, and the Yank swung his sabre down. The pommel smashed into Fell's skull, and he toppled from the saddle.

When he came to, the melee was over and he was lying on his back to one side of the shattered breastworks. The bodies of the dead lay all about in the frozen pools of their own blood. He sat up slowly, his skull soft as butter, and put a hand to his face, which burned like fire. Sticky blood came away on his fingers: a gash stretched from his scalp to his chin, barely missing the left eye. He couldn't understand how he was still alive. But Max had seen him fall and dragged him clear, or he'd have been trampled to death.

Max! Half cut to pieces and shot through the meat of one arm, he found two horses and put Fell in the saddle. The pike was lost, Hood's army in rout. They snuck through the woods, dodging Federals all night, till they found some of Chalmers' forces, scattered like chaff before the wind; and with them they fought rear-guard all the way to the Duck River. The Yanks drove them from every position they took, but the main force –disheartened, disorganized, a rabble dressed in rags and half of them barefoot –managed to get away through the ice and snow. Some of them would fight again, but anyone could see the cause was lost. For Fell's wound, there'd been no medical attention; the scar would be broad and deep.

iii.

The kid's face swam before his eyes, and he thought he heard the kid laugh, that harsh mocking laugh that made you want to kill him, just to shut him up. Just like back in Indian Territory... Fell had camped near a small river. It was a cool, pleasant night and he was sitting by the fire after supper, smoking a cigar and trying not to think too hard. He heard a rider coming a long way off and hoped the man would pass on by; he didn't want company. But a stranger rode up, nodding pleasantly. "Howdy."

"Evening," Fell said.

"I seen your campfire," the stranger said. "Mind if I set with you a spell?"

"Suit yourself," Fell said.

The man swung down easily enough, though something about him suggested a city dweller. Maybe it was his clothes –they were newish, and clean, like a man who makes his living in saloons and dance halls. Fell didn't trust him.

The man crouched down by the fire and grinned. "Thank you kindly," he said. "Truth is, I was concerned about gettin' ambushed."

"Not too many Indians around here," Fell said.

"No, but Hell," the man said. "White men are worse than Indians when it comes to thievin'."

Fell just nodded, uninterested. Without thinking too hard about it, there was something about the man he didn't like.

The stranger took a cigar from his shirt pocket and lit it. "Nope," he said. "The white man is the true savage. I don't care what people say. The Indian fights the invader. He kills the dispossessor of his land –and of his soul. But the white man kills for money. And when he ain't killing for money, he kills out of plain meanness –for the pleasure of killing, you might say."

Fell didn't want to listen to this. In a flat, even tone, he said, "You're a philosopher."

But the other man just laughed, laughed good and hard, as if Fell had said something truly funny. "Oh, no," he said. "Or anyway, it's not metaphysics that interest me. Let's say I'm a social theorist. I don't look beyond what's right here on earth."

He reached for his hip-pocket. Fell watched him closely, but he only brought out a small metal flask. He took a sip, proffered it. Fell shook his head. He didn't drink with strangers.

"No?" the other man said. "Sir, you don't know what you're missing. This here is Kentucky sour mash, finest grade. Well, to your health!" He drank again.

"No, sir, that's the real thing," he went on, louder now, warmed by the drink. "Not like the rotgut they sell in these towns. Why, that stuff is nothing but poison! I've seen men go blind who drank too much of it... What's that?"

He jumped to his feet with a clatter, looking away toward the river, one hand on his gun. "Someone's coming!"

Fell shook his head. "I didn't hear anything."

"I'm telling you someone's coming," the man insisted, excitement rising in his voice. "By God, I ain't gettin' bushwhacked..."

"Calm down," Fell said. "There's nothing out there."

He heard a metallic click behind him: the hammer cocking back on a gun.

"Fell, you're right about that," a familiar voice said. "There *ain't* nobody over there."

Anger boiled inside him but he didn't move, just said evenly, coldly, "Sanford."

The stranger stepped lightly to his horse and drew out a rifle. "Alright, Mr. Fell," he said, without a trace of animosity. "Take out your sidearm there and toss it aside." He trained the rifle on Fell's midsection.

Fell didn't have much choice. He did as he was told, looking up into the stranger's eyes. "Nice company you keep."

"Just doin' a job," the stranger said.

"I'll remember that," Fell said. "When I find you later."

One corner of the stranger's mouth curled, but he didn't answer.

That was when the kid stepped into the light, laughing his mocking laugh. "Look out, Pinkie," he said. "I think ol' Fell is tryin' to scare you."

"Pinkie," Fell said. "Pinkie Loughton, I guess. Where's your ring, Pinkie?"

The stranger grinned. "Why, it's right here in my shirt pocket," he said. He shifted the rifle to his other hand, fished something out of his pocket and slipped it on his little finger: a silver ring in the shape of a skull, with two rubies for eyes. "Truth is," he went on, "I didn't want you to recognize me too soon."

"Oh, I know a snake when I see one," Fell said.

Pinkie's eyes narrowed but otherwise his expression didn't change. Fell had heard of him: a small-time gambler and dry-gulcher. He did most of his work in alleys and around corners, with the butt of a gun. Just the sort the kid liked to pal around with.

"Ol' Fell, he's still the same," the kid said. He held a Colt revolver in each hand, trained on Fell's chest. "He comes on tough, even when he's in a bad spot." He laughed again, mocking. "And you're in a bad spot now, old man."

Fell forced himself to stay cool. "I been in worse," he said.

The kid's face flushed. "To Hell with you, *old man*," he snapped. "You still think you're *pretty tough*. Well, you shouldn't have come out here after me. You should've let bygones be bygones."

"Sanford, you killed my best friend," Fell said. "Killed him so you could rob us. The world ain't big enough for you to hide. Sooner or later, I'll get you."

The kid laughed again but it was forced, full of barely-contained anger. "You'll get me? *You* will get *me*? Have you gone loco, Fell? You're setting there unarmed, looking down the barrel of my gun. You're going to die here, old man! I'm going to shoot you down like a mad dog, and leave your body where it falls."

"You never were one for a fair fight, kid."

Pinkie smirked at that. The kid flew into a rage: "To Hell with you, old man! You're dead! You hear me? You're *dead!* But I'll make you beg for your life before I kill you."

Fell smiled a little, despite himself. The kid aimed one of the guns at Fell's head: "Crawl, old man. Plead for your life and maybe I'll spare it."

Fell just looked at him.

"C'mon, old man!" the kid said. His hand was shaking. "C'mon!"

He swung the barrel down and fired. The bullet kicked up dust near Fell's boot and ricocheted away. He aimed at Fell's face again. "Come on!"

"Sanford," Pinkie said lowly. "I think somebody's coming up the trail."

"Shut up," the kid snapped. He fired again. The bullet sang past Fell's ear. Fell didn't move.

"Sanford, I'm telling you," Pinkie said. "Somebody's coming."

"I don't give a damn," the kid said. "Old man, I told you to beg for your life."

"Sonny boy," Fell said, "I seen thousands die in the War while you were still in short pants. Your pop-gun don't impress me much."

The kid's face was so red it was almost black. But Pinkie said, "Sanford, I'm gettin' out of here."

"Go to Hell," the kid said. Pinkie shrugged. He swung into the saddle, turned the horse and rode away into the dark.

"Nice choice in men," Fell said. "Reliable."

The kid didn't answer, his face clenched with hate. But he cocked his head, listening, and now Fell heard it, too: riders, coming toward the camp.

"Well, sonny boy," Fell said. "Your playmate is gone. What now?"

The kid turned on him, quivering with rage. "Go to Hell..."

He pulled the trigger, the barrel point-blank in Fell's face.

iv.

When Fell came to, he wasn't sure how he was still alive. It was dark and he didn't have any idea where he was. All he knew was that his head hurt, bad. When he tried to move, it hurt a lot worse. He sat up anyway and put a hand to his head. A poultice or something covered his right eye. When he touched it a wave of nausea went through him and he took his hand away.

The feeling passed and he just sat there, trying to remember. Little by little it came back: the kid... The kid had gotten the drop on him in camp... He'd shot him, point-blank.

Nothing was very clear... There'd been the other one, too; what was his name? And goddamn but he was lucky to be alive! But how had he gotten... here?

He tried to get up but the nausea went through him again, pain stabbing through his head. Retching, he put out a hand, touched something and felt of it: hide. A hide tent. Indians –Indians had found him. He got to his hands and knees, started to get to his feet, but black spots boiled before his eyes and he fell, unconscious.

When he came to again it was daylight outside, some of the light filtering into the tent. This time he just lay there for a while, keeping still and letting it come to him. The kid... Pinkie, that was the other one... The Indian tent... Indians had found him. They'd saved him, for some reason of their own. He wondered dimly about that but his thoughts faded away again.

He slept, awoke, slept again. The next time he woke it was dark, then light again; dark once more. He awoke again, saw black eyes looking at him –an Indian woman, neither young nor old, frowning a bit but not unkindly. She looked thoughtfully into his face for a long moment, and went away.

He waited, only a little apprehensive. Of course his gun belt was gone. But they hadn't tended his wounds just to kill him now. Sure enough, in a minute or two the woman was back, with food and a gourd of water.

He ate as if starved, slowed only by the pain when he chewed. But once he'd eaten, a terrible fatigue came over him, and he lay down again, his head throbbing dully. In a while the woman returned.

"Food good?" she asked.

"Yes," he said. "Thank you. You're very kind."

"No talk," she said. "Rest now. Tonight grandmother talk to you."

"Okay," he said. Grandmother: she would be the medicine-woman. As he fell asleep again, he wondered what she would say.

Grandmother was very old. How old, perhaps even she didn't know; maybe a hundred, maybe more. Her face was as wrinkled as a dried apple, and she made not one unnecessary movement, as if husbanding her strength; but her eyes sparkled with keen intelligence, and Fell could tell she missed nothing.

She was sitting by the fire when they brought him before her, and she looked him over carefully, as if considering the results of her work. He held his hat in his hand and after one look into her face he went painfully down on one knee, as he might have before a queen. With the faintest of smiles she made a gesture that he should stand, and said, "How are you called?"

"Abraham Fell," he said simply.

She nodded, and continued to examine him for a time. Her expression was grave. Finally she said, "How do you feel?"

"Better," Fell said. He went on: "You saved my life. I am beholden to you."

Without acknowledging his thanks, she said, "When the men brought you here I thought you would die. We heard the raven's cry of the *Ka'lanu ahkyeli'ski* and knew it hungered for your soul. But I saw that which follows you like a second shadow. A ghosts walks with you, haunts your every step. Did you know that, Abraham Fell?"

Something cold passed through him, a sort of awe mixed with dread... As if it were a question, he said, "Max?"

"Is that the ghost?" she asked.

"He was my friend," Fell said. "We served together in the War. He saved my life... I couldn't save his."

"So you have given your life to avenge him." It wasn't a question. He couldn't meet her eyes, just nodded and said, "Yes."

After a silence, she said, "Hate is strong in you. It keeps you alive, but it has taken your heart. You bear an awful burden, Abraham Fell. Yet I could not let you die, else there had been two ghosts. Perhaps... Perhaps you will wish I had."

He had faced death many times, fought and killed and never been afraid, but now fear touched him, sank cold claws into his heart. He opened his mouth but found no words to speak.

She looked away, into the night, something like regret in her face. "The *Ka'lanu ahkyeli'ski* had already claimed your soul. I could not drive it off, as I sometimes have with others. But by a terrible bargain I saved your life. You are his now, and he, a part of you. I do not know... just what will come, nor what become of you. But you may seek your vengeance, and, should you find it, lay the ghost of your friend. After that..."

He nodded as if he understood. He didn't, or not well, and dreaded fuller understanding. All he knew was his fear.

"Stay with us until the full moon," she said, "and build back your strength; but then you must go. The spirit now within you is terrible: it sows violence, and reaps despair and death. My people need peace."

"As you wish," Fell said. "And thank you."

"Thank me not yet," she answered, "but abide a time, and see."

It was over a week until the full moon. For the first few days he slept a great deal. The wound began to heal. His right eye was dead, blinded, and the bullet had seamed the flesh, taken a little bone. He could not imagine how the kid had missed, and failed to finish the job. Had those riders on the trail spooked him, had he run, believing Fell dead? He couldn't know. Eventually he stopped thinking about it. He was alive, that was the main thing. He still had one good eye.

What the old woman had said worried him a lot more. Once, when he was younger, he might have dismissed it all as Indian superstition, childish mummery. Experience had eaten at his skepticism, and undermined his confidence that he understood the world. Some frightful reality lurked behind the old woman's words, something it would be folly to deny; nor did he believe she had told him all. The other Indians treated him kindly, but they kept their distance, and remained aloof. After a time he remarked that no child ever came near him. The younger women who brought him food struggled to master their fear; in the faces of the older ones was a sort of pity tinged with sadness. He found both disturbing.

As he got stronger, he began to take walks away from camp. When he was alone he had only his thoughts to worry him. The Indians returned his gun; the familiar weight of the gunbelt around his hips was a certain comfort. This part of the Territory was wide and empty, almost barren, and it was good to breathe in the clean air, the scent of prairie grass, to feel the touch of the incessant wind. It was good to be alive. But as his strength returned, and the great yellow moon waxed, he longed to be moving again.

They brought him before the old woman the night the moon was full. "Abraham Fell," she said. "Your wound heals."

"Yes, ma'am," he said awkwardly, unsure how to address her. "Your medicine is strong."

"Bad medicine," she said. "Are you well enough to ride?"

"Yes."

"Then tomorrow morning you ride out. We will give you food and water for several days."

He nodded. "You are very kind. I thank you."

"May the Great Spirit guide you and protect you. Your road is hard, Abraham Fell, and I do not envy you. But do not return among us."

He nodded. They led him away.

In the dawn light the Indian camp fell behind him. He rode west, for something told him that was the way. He didn't question it. His shadow stretched before him, strangely fluid and distorted. But he was glad to be in the saddle again, and rode easily, little bothered by his wound.

v.

That night he camped in a little grove near a spring. Plagued by memory, he rolled himself in a blanket and waited for sleep. It did not come easily, and when it did, was filled with vicious dreams of bloodshed and murder. But with the dawn came a certain calm and he saddled up and rode on.

Indian Territory: the land was wide and empty. Fell liked it that way. He kept to himself, fighting shy of the world. The kid might have been somewhere along the way but he didn't think so. In point of fact he *knew* it: some strange intuition that he could not question told him the kid wasn't there, that his prey –how had he come to use that word? –was ahead, somewhere out West.

The day passed, and as night came on, he camped again. After a meager supper, salt pork and beans, he sat thinking it out. The kid was out West, that much he knew; but where? He'd left Fell for dead, and had no reason to think himself followed. San Francisco? Maybe –but a big town wasn't his style: too many people, too much law. The kid would rather rob you while you slept, shoot you in the back. Easy money was his way. The mining country? It was wide open, had plenty of pickings. But it was big: Arizona, Colorado, California... That was a lot of ground to cover.

He threw the last of the coffee on the ground and stretched out on his back, looking up at the stars. He'd find him. Right now, it was good out here, away from people...

The sound of hoofs broke his reverie. He sat up, hand on his gun. Two men rode into the dying light. They were dirty and tough-looking, riding tired, underfed horses. One was a little smaller than the other, with hard eyes and a thin beard. "Howdy, stranger," he said.

Fell knew they were trouble. He looked from one to the other, and said evenly, "Howdy."

The second man didn't speak at all as his eyes looked this way and that, taking in Fell and the camp. Fell waited.

"We been ridin' all day," the smaller man said, "and when we seen your fire, we thought maybe you'd be kindly enough to share your supper with us."

"Supper's over," Fell said. "As you can plainly see."

"And you wouldn't have anything to help us out, say, in them saddlebags?"

"Afraid not," Fell said. Now the second man was staring at him, his mouth hanging open and fear crawling over his face. *What in Hell?* Fell thought.

But the first man shook his head. "Did you hear that, Abel? Turned us down flat. And yet, from that hat and the twang in his voice, I'm guessing he's a Southern man. I heard Southerners were known for their hospitality," he said, addressing Fell.

"Guess you heard wrong," Fell said.

"Well, *that's* not very hospitable. You know, Abel," he went on, "I never did hold with Secessionists. Seems to me Grant and Sherman and all done a good job getting rid of most of 'em." He pulled a sawed-off shotgun from a holster on his saddle. "Maybe we ought to help finish the job."

Fell's skin was prickling. He already disliked this jasper, irritated by his insulting tone, and the mention of Sherman. But now rage flashed through him, and suddenly he wanted to kill the man. Something inside him pushed him to – urged it, almost irresistible –and laughed, in an awful, sickening glee of blood-lust and hunger. He held onto himself, fighting, as this –*thing* –tried to take control of him, like an animal smashing against its cage. His sight swam in a red haze. Teeth clenched, he said, "You two better ride out of here if you don't want to die."

The one who'd done all the talking just laughed –but now his face was a dead man's. "Hey, Johnny Reb," he said, through lips that were rotting away. "You got it all wrong. You're the one who's gonna die."

Fell had known war, and he was fast with a gun; but he'd never been so fast before. He brought up his Colt and fired two shots. The slugs took the bearded man in the heart before he could fire the sawed-off. His finger squeezed the trigger in a death-spasm, and the spray of shot stung his horse; it reared up, throwing him off, and galloped away. Shaking with fear, the one called Abel went to draw. Fell swung the muzzle and shot him in the throat. Abel dropped his pistol and clutched at the wound, then fell from the saddle. The horse whinnied, eyes rolling; it turned and followed the first.

Fell got to his feet, shaken and flushed with adrenaline. The bearded man lay unmoving, crumpled on the ground. Abel was still alive: on his knees, moving feebly, he held one hand to his throat, choking, terror on his face. Blood ran over his fingers and down his chest, soaking his shirt. His lips moved and blood bubbled from between them. Somewhere nearby, a crow cawed loudly. Abel tried to say something but couldn't get it out. He pitched over and lay still. The crow cawed again.

Fell stood looking at the two dead men. He felt strangely empty, as if a void had opened up inside him. The crow kept cawing, louder and louder, insistent. Not far away, a coyote howled, the sound lonesome and timid, as if the creature feared for its life. The crow cawed once more and fell silent.

Fell felt no remorse. These men were killers, and he knew they would have killed him. Their deaths had no meaning, but he felt old, and tired. And why had the one called Abel been so afraid?

His horse stirred uneasily. He picked up the dead men's guns and stripped them of their cartridge belts. The sawed-off looked particularly useful. He suspected now that there would be more killing, maybe a lot more. He stowed it in a saddlebag and went back to the dying fire. The faces of the dead men were pale in the moonlight, spectres in an empty land.

As he stared bitterly into the embers, something slid back down inside his skin –something sated and content, like a wild beast that has fed, and would rest. He'd almost been expecting it. The void was gone –filled again –but he felt a nameless horror of what he was becoming, or had become. The two gunmen he'd killed were gone down to whatever Hell awaited them; but he knew now that he carried his own Hell inside him. They had died as men, but he was no longer entirely human.

When dawn came he made breakfast, saddled up and rode on. The two bodies he left where they lay. Such men didn't deserve a burial; the coyotes and vultures could have them. He looked back once and saw six or seven of the hungry birds already circling.

He rode easily, alert but pensive. What had happened the night before was slowly settling through him. Though he'd lived a violent life, he did not think himself a violent man; though he had killed many times, he had never taken pleasure in killing. He killed when it was necessary, and when it wasn't necessary, he did what he could to avoid it. And except when the dead were scoundrels, like those two last night, he usually felt a kind of remorse.

He still remembered the first man he'd killed, early in the War. He was just a kid back then, freshly commissioned and nominally in command of men who knew infinitely more of war than he did. They'd ridden out on patrol, trying to reconnoiter the enemy flank, and as they forded a low river, Yankee skirmishers fell on them. There was a rattle of musket fire and the man next to him dropped, shot from the saddle. Fighting his own fear, Fell spurred his horse forward and drew his service revolver. A Yank who didn't look sixteen jabbed a bayonet at his guts. Fell shot him in the heart. The expression of pain and sorrow on the boy's face imprinted itself on his memory, and when the fight was over, back in camp, he'd gone away from the others and wept.

Since then... he didn't know how many men he'd killed. War hardens a man, and the confusion of battle is such that when it's over you don't rightly know what you've done. But now...

He'd thought that avenging Max would be the only killing that would ever give him pleasure. He'd imagined it many times, rehearsed it, as it were... And he'd wondered, more than once, if when it was over he'd have the strength to carry on; or if it would be time to die. He didn't know, figuring only time would tell.

All that was changed now. Everything was changed. What had the old medicine-woman said? "You are his now, and he a part of you." Was he a slave to its will —to its blood-lust? Was he still the master of himself, and his actions? He remembered, ill at ease, the almost shocking speed with which he'd drawn and fired, the uncanny accuracy with which the shots had found their mark. He remembered, too, how *it* wanted him to kill, pushed him to do it. The other... lusted for blood, and sated itself upon death. Perhaps it fed upon men's souls. Now, it seemed, Fell should have to supply it with its fearsome provender.

vi.

The way became dry and dusty, the country turning gradually to desert. He headed west-northwest, thinking to cross one of the stagecoach trails and follow it. But soon his food was running low, though he didn't seem to require much, as if he lived on the idea of vengeance alone. He stretched what provisions he had hunting and trapping, but that took time, and he wanted to keep moving. Finally everything was so short that he had no choice; he had to stop in the next town.

As it turned out, that was another day's ride. The sun was sinking low ahead of him when he saw it, and he hoped he wouldn't have to wait till morning. Better to get what he needed and keep moving. Towns were their own kind of trouble.

But as he neared the town something came over him, a weird feeling he'd never known before. The ramshackle buildings ahead seemed to waver in their outlines, for a moment become unreal, and a sudden morbidity invested everything, as if death were everywhere, all around. A rounded outcropping of rock leered at him with the features of a skull; from the corners of his eyes –for now *his dead eye saw again* – he saw headstones and graves, which when he turned to look were gone; and from nowhere vultures appeared, kiting easily in the sky, and wheeling in great arcs above him and the town ahead.

It had one dirt street and a handful of weather-beaten wooden buildings that had never known paint. There was a stage stop with bleared windows, a livery stable, a mercantile, a saloon. One or two of the structures had a boardwalk. No one was on the street. He stopped in front of the mercantile, tied up and went in.

The door creaked, a tin bell rattled and the shopkeeper came through a curtain from the back. He was a smallish man, balding, with a tidy beard. He was smiling and the smile stayed fixed but something came into his eyes when he looked at Fell. Fell noted that, unsure what the man saw. The man nodded emphatically as Fell told his few needs, then scurried about gathering up the order, still nodding.

Somehow, the shopkeeper was afraid of him. Fell wondered at that, for he had spoken quietly and civilly. But after all he was a stranger. Vaguely irritated by the other man's craven servility, he turned to look out the window, but his glance fell upon a mirror. Startled, he stepped closer.

There was his face, dirty and unshaven beneath the battered cavalry hat, but something was –*wrong*. The eye gleamed sharply from a hollowed orbit; and he saw plainly the skull beneath the skin. His sight blurred. A death's head gazed back from the glass. He blinked, and it was gone.

Shaken, he turned away. Was this it, then? What that Abel had seen, and now this man? Was this what others saw when they looked at him?

The shopkeeper was cringing behind the counter. Distracted, his thoughts confused, Fell paid and left. He stowed the goods in his saddlebags and stood patting the horse's neck, musing. Already, the sun was setting, casting a bloody glow in the dusty windows. He'd thought to move on, but his throat was dry. The saloon was only a few steps away. Almost against his will he turned toward it.

The few men all looked up when he walked in. He glanced around and went to the bar. Distrust was written in the barkeep's face, but he brought Fell his whiskey and went back to where he'd been –probably to be closer to his gun. Fell ignored him. He swallowed the whiskey and gestured for another. The second didn't make him feel any better. He leaned on his elbows, staring down at the cracked varnish of the bar, avoiding the mirror. Something stirred within him, as if impatient.

He heard a step. A man stood beside him.

With an evil presentiment, he looked up. The man was staring hard at him. He was fairly tall, sunburnt and hard-looking, with a star pinned to his chest.

"Can I help you, marshal?" Fell said.

The marshal's eyes flinched but his voice was cool: "New in town?"

"You know I am," Fell said.

"Then you may not know we don't want trouble here."

Fell looked toward the barkeep and pointed to his glass. "Fine with me," he said, not looking at the marshal. "I don't want none, either."

"Good," the marshal said. His voice was tight. Fell could tell he was trying to master himself. "So you won't mind riding out when you finish your drink."

Irritation flashed through him but he fought it. "Marshal, I just rode in half an hour ago, to buy supplies. A man can't have a drink in this town?"

"You've had your drink," the marshal said. His hand moved to his gun. "Now ride out."

Fell straightened, looking at him. He couldn't believe what was happening. He glanced around. Everyone in the bar was staring at them. Fell shook his head. He didn't want trouble with a lawman. But the marshal seemed to mistake him: he drew himself up and slipped the thong from his gun. "Ride out, or shoot it out," he said, jaw clenched.

"Have it your way," Fell said. He turned toward the barkeep, reaching in one pocket. "Forget it," the marshal said. "Lawrence! Put this man's drinks on my bill. Now go," he said to Fell. "And don't come back."

"Friendly town," Fell said. He walked to the door, skin crawling. He was angry now, and something inside him liked the anger –something that, laughing, pricked and goaded his pride. Something that wanted him to kill. He paused in the doorway, one hand on a panel of the swinging door. Behind him, he heard a voice say, "Drifter trash." He turned, saw the barkeep fumble beneath the bar, saw the marshal's hand on his gun –saw the fear on their faces –fear, and loathing. It was too much. He almost snapped. He wanted to *kill* –kill them *all* – draw his gun and shoot them down –leave not a soul alive. *He needed to kill* –spill their blood –the need like a spring that can't hold, that has to let go...

He plunged through the door, into the dusky street, and staggered to his horse. As he rode out, shaken and sickened, something inside him raged and raved in frustration.

vii.

The stage station was a low, one-storey building with a yard and a corral. When Fell was still a couple hundred yards away, a man with a rifle stepped out the front door and stood waiting in the shade of the awning. No doubt another man was inside, behind the window. Fell kept his pace, taking in everything. The spot was lonely: nothing in sight, and no dust on the horizon.

Inside him, something stirred, restless.

He nodded to the man with the rifle as he rode up, and swung down from the saddle. The man returned the nod, his eyes cool and appraising, before scanning the trail again. Fell waited.

"Help you?" the man said at length.

"I'd like my horse fed and watered," Fell said. "And I'd like some hot food myself."

The rifleman studied him. "Okay," he said, then asked, "You here for the stage?"

"No," Fell said. "I'll be riding out after I've eaten, and rested a little."

The other man weighed this a moment. "Go on in. I'll have my boys take care of your horse."

"Much obliged," Fell said.

Inside it was cool and dim, with a stamped-earth floor, and some rough tables and benches. As he'd guessed, a second man with a rifle was keeping a lookout through the one window. Fell nodded to him and sat down. The other man returned the nod, looking closely at him. Fell took off his hat and wiped his face on his sleeve.

A woman came out of the kitchen. She had a kindly but anxious look. "Help you?" she said, wiping her hands. There was a pleasing twang to her voice.

"I'd like some food, ma'am," Fell said. "Steak and eggs if you've got it, or whatever you've got that's good and hot."

"Steak, eggs, hashbrowns, grits?" she said.

"Sounds delicious, ma'am. And some water, if you please. Hot and dry out there."

She brought him a bucket and gourd, went to the window and looked out. The man shook his head. She went back to the kitchen. In a few minutes he could smell the food cooking. He drank a little and sat quietly, trying not to think, satisfied just to rest for a spell.

In a bit she came back with the food. She set it before him, and went to the window again. "It's late?" he heard her say to the lookout.

"Not yet... but we ought to see something by now," the man replied.

Fell had not been thinking about the stage. He set to the food like a starving man. Turning, she saw, and smiled. "Everything alright?"

"Delicious, ma'am," Fell said.

There were hoofbeats in the yard, and the man with the rifle tensed. The woman hurried back to the bar, stepping behind it and reaching out something. Fell heard a metallic click, then another. Shotgun, he thought, suddenly tense himself.

"Who is it, Jed?" the woman said, her voice low.

"Four men," the man at the window answered. "I don't know any of 'em. Been ridin' hard. Fine horses. I don't think I like this. And there's dust down the trail. That'll be the stage."

He glanced at Fell, as if to size up what he was doing. Fell went on eating as if he hadn't noticed.

"They're a-talkin' to Alvin," Jed said, speaking to the woman without looking away. "Can't tell what about. Wonder if I ought to go out there."

"You stay put at that window," the woman said. "And keep your finger on the trigger. That's what Alvin told you to do."

Jed didn't answer, just kept looking through the window, rifle ready.

Fell didn't like this a bit. Whatever was on that stage wasn't any of his business, but these people were expecting trouble and he was sitting almost in the crossfire.

He finished his food and pushed the plate away, poured himself a cup of coffee and sat still, waiting. They could hear the stage now, the rumbling wheels and creaking wood, the horses, slowing now to a trot. Fell thought he heard voices too, raised in contention, but nothing clear. The stage rolled into the yard.

A shout went up, and a gun cracked. Jed straightened, the rifle to his shoulder, and fired through the window. Fell heard more gunfire outside. Jed cranked the Winchester, jacking another shell into the chamber, and fired again. Bullets smashed into wood, throwing splinters, and he stumbled back, knocking over a chair and falling to the floor.

The woman screamed and started around the bar but now Fell was on his feet, gun in his hand. "Stay down!" he hissed. She looked in his eyes and did as he told her.

He moved to the door like a ghost, the weird blood-lust on him now, winding up his nerves, quickening his reflexes. Outside, the man with the rifle lay sprawled in the dirt, perfectly still, and not far away another man lay crumpled on the ground –one of the outlaws, no doubt. The stage driver was dead, too. The other three riders had the stage's doors open and were covering the passengers with their guns.

Fell drew aim, but hesitated –this wasn't his fight – though something inside him pushed him to shoot them down where they stood. Behind him, he heard the woman wail. He glanced back. She'd crept out on her hands and knees to where Jed lay, blood soaking his shirt. "No, no," she sobbed.

One of the outlaws heard it too. He looked around, saw Fell, and swung the muzzle of his gun. Fell shot him between the eyes. The man fell back like a broken doll, into the dust. The other two turned quick, muzzles seeking their target. One dropped to one knee and fired. Fell fired at the one still standing, two shots in the chest, so fast it sounded like one, even as the first man's shot slapped into the doorframe next to him with a spray of splinters. Fell swung his gun and fired again, twice, but the outlaw rolled, and the slugs hit him in the left thigh and knee. He doubled up in pain.

Fell strode into the hot sunlight, straight to him. He could feel the bloodlust raging like a fever. The outlaw's gun had tumbled away, out of reach. He looked at it, then at Fell, both hands clutching his knee, fingers covered in blood. What he saw in Fell's face made him very afraid. "Don't... Don't kill me," he stammered.

Fell didn't want to kill him. He fought it. His right hand shook, holding the gun.

"Please..." the wounded man said.

Fell looked around –at the other dead outlaw, at the stage driver's body, sprawled over the seat, and back at the station, where the man called Alvin lay dead in front, and he could still hear the woman sobbing. Inside him, something leapt and gibbered and frothed at the mouth, its need beating upon his consciousness.

It was too strong. He pulled the trigger and shot the wounded man in the heart.

Calm descended upon him. He broke open the revolver, discarded the empty casings, and reloaded.

Somewhere, a crow was cawing.

viii.

Jed wasn't dead. That was good, anyway; but he'd caught two slugs and would take some time to heal. His wife – her name was Annie –was the most grateful, but she hadn't seen much of the killing. The others, the passengers from the stage, all thanked him sincerely enough, but he saw the fear in their eyes –and loathing, too. He couldn't blame them. He'd executed a man while they looked on, a man who'd asked for mercy; and he'd executed him not because he was a murderous bandit but because something Fell carried inside him wanted blood spilled and souls on which to feed.

So he rode out, saddle bags full of provisions that Annie insisted he take. She and Jed were safe enough, he figured, until the next stage arrived. He left it to the others to bury the dead.

He rode west, following the stage trail. It was good to be alone, out under the great open sky. He didn't want to be around people. There was no one to kill, that way, and he didn't have to see in their eyes what they saw in him.

Crossing the broken, rocky land was slow, monotonous. After a time he lost track of the days. They didn't matter; he wasn't in a hurry. The miles went by easily. He guessed he was covering thirty-five to forty a day, taking it easy on his horse, just going steadily along. The nights were something else. It began maybe four or five nights after the shoot-out at the stage station. He lay rolled in his blanket near the dying fire when something stirred inside him –something restless, which hungered. Something that wanted him to kill, that it might feed.

Thereafter it was with him every night; and every night it was a little stronger, a little more forceful, slowly bending him to its will. And he knew that, in the end, it would be stronger than him.

Unless he made a deal...

For he, too, wanted blood. Thereafter, he opened his heart to the Other, bared the hate that seethed and festered within, the desire for vengeance like an open wound –telling it, Help me –Lead me to him –Show me the way and I will kill for you...

He didn't know if the Other listened, didn't know if it accepted the pact. He couldn't know... but the nights were calm again, though watchful, and expectant.

Ahead, the mountains reared up against the sky, majestic and proud. He watched them grow a little larger each day as he followed the trail, stopping once in a while at a stage station. He never stayed long, just ate a hot meal, bought supplies and rode out. He spoke little, made no acquaintances, minded his own affairs. There was no trouble.

It must have been mid-afternoon when he saw the town ahead. He'd already fought shy of several and thought to do the same, when a sort of compulsion came over him. His will sapped, he knew, without question, he was stopping in this town. He wondered why, but he just accepted it. There didn't seem anything else to do.

He rode past a couple adobe huts, empty shells where tumbleweeds lodged, and reached the town's outskirts. If it had a name he didn't notice it. As he passed the cemetery the weird came upon him, strong. He looked down into the ground and saw the dead buried there. Some were dressed in their Sunday best, lying in a wooden box; and others lay rolled in a blanket with their boots on, held close in the embrace of the earth. Some had been dead a long time, others not so long, and one or two had just been interred. He looked from one to another, unsure whether he saw the past or the future. But now he came into the town.

Although he could have sworn he'd seen movement from some ways off –folks on the street, going about their business –now the streets were silent and deserted. Had they sensed his approach, and hidden themselves away? He rode slowly down the middle of the dusty street looking left and right at nothing, past the stage office and next to it a bank, a dry goods store, a livery stable, a hotel... the marshal's office... The place might have been a ghost town. At the cross street, he saw, off to one side, a saloon, the Bon Ton. He turned toward it, somehow knowing that was where he was supposed to go.

A horse was tied up in front. He dismounted, tied his own horse next to it. The other horse looked at him and rolled its eyes; it tried to shy away. He stood for a moment there in the sun, then turned to the door.

A man was drinking alone at a table by the window. Fell went to the bar. The barkeep came toward him, a gaunt man whose oiled hair made him look like an undertaker. When he saw Fell, he blinked but his expression remained fixed, as if he didn't like what he saw but controlled himself with an effort.

"Whiskey," Fell said. It was as if a ghost had spoken.

The barkeep poured a shot and went away. Fell drank some, then stared down into the glass, wondering why he was there. The weird was strong on him now: when he raised his eye to the mirror, a skull stared back. He drank off the rest and called for more, not looking up again.

In the back of the room a clock chimed three times. Behind him he heard the man at the table get up and go to the bar. The barkeep said, "Something else for you, Pinkie?"

"Nope," the man answered. "I'll be back later, see if I can get a game going..."

Fell's gun was in his hand as he turned toward the two men. "Pinkie?" he said. "Pinkie *Loughton?*"

The man at the bar turned toward him and Fell saw fear cross his face. His hand went toward his gun and stopped.

"What's the matter, Pinkie?" Fell said. "Seen a ghost?"

The barkeep was backing away, out of the line of fire.

"Abraham Fell," Pinkie said softly, as if in disbelief.

"In the flesh," Fell said. "Guess you didn't figure on runnin' into me here."

"Listen, Fell," Pinkie began. "That whole job, well, it weren't none of *my* grudge..."

"Hold on, Pinkie," Fell said. "I think we ought to talk outside." He nodded toward the door. "Let's go –and keep your hands where I can see 'em. You don't have to worry, I ain't gonna shoot you –*in the back.*"

They went out the door, Pinkie first, Fell covering him. Outside, in the blinding sunlight, the street was just as empty as before. Pinkie stopped on the boardwalk; he started to say something again. Fell gave him a nudge with his gun barrel.

"Out in the street, Pinkie," he said. "Don't want any accidents to happen."

Inside him, something restive strained to be set free. Fell had to fight the urge to gun down Pinkie right then. Instead, gritting his teeth, he said, "Tell me about Sanford."

Pinkie was sweating. He knew he was in a bad spot and picked his words carefully: "I ain't seen that... that little bastard in maybe a month. I rode with him for a spell but I got sick of... of his games. You got to believe me, I didn't cotton to what he done to you, neither! It was just a job... and even then, he like to didn't pay me. Nothing personal, Fell, it was just a job."

"Where is he now?"

"I don't know! He went on west... He always had all of these schemes, none of 'em honest..."

"West to where?"

"Mining country... Anyways, that's what he said he was gonna do. I told him I didn't want to go. I was sick of him, the little rat..."

Fell laughed at that, the sound harsh in his throat. "I see," he said. "And all the things you done with him, you're regretful of 'em now... Contrite, even."

Pinkie looked unsure how to answer: "Well, yeah! I mean... I didn't like being associated with him."

"I can see that," Fell said. "But what's done is done."

Pinkie's eyes narrowed. His hand moved toward his gun. Blood-lust flared inside Fell; his finger tightened on the trigger. With an effort, he mastered himself. The man before him already looked spectral.

"Alright, Pinkie," he said. "I'm sure everything you've told me is the Gospel truth, so I'm gonna give you a chance." He holstered his gun.

A nervous smile played over Pinkie's face, even as a wolfish look came into his eyes. But he hesitated.

"You and me got a score to settle," Fell said quietly. "When you're ready."

Pinkie licked his lips and went for his gun. With uncanny speed, Fell's was already in his hand, firing. Pinkie spun in place and crumpled onto the dusty street, his free hand clutched to the wounds in his chest.

A rush of exultation went through Fell, followed by calm. He crouched down by the body and picked up the dead man's hand and its little ring like a skull, with rubies for eyes. Fell slipped it off the finger and put it in his pocket, then stood up and looked around. The street was still empty. Fell shrugged. He mounted up, and rode slowly out of town.

Somewhere behind him a crow was cawing, loudly.

Abraham Fell rode due west, the town whose name he'd never learned falling behind him, to disappear. He rode slumped in the saddle, his good eye watching the trail and the horizon automatically. Inside him, the Other was quiet, sated and at rest, but Fell was low, and heavy at heart. He'd killed his man, but the fact gave him no pleasure and no satisfaction, eased no burden of the spirit. True, Pinkie had done him wrong, but he'd only been the kid's accomplice. Fell would've had a quarrel with him had they happened to meet, but he would never have sought out the gunman on his own. What the man had done hadn't really warranted killing him. And Fell found himself appalled at what he'd become, appalled and more than a little afraid.

He thought of Max, for had it not been his own consuming desire for vengeance that had led the old medicine-woman to do what she'd done? But Max had become vague to him; he could no longer clearly recall his friend's face, or the sound of his voice. He was like a shadow now, fading irrevocably. What remained perfectly clear was the memory of the kid, his smirking expression, and hateful, mocking laugh. Hate remained when all else passed away. Helpless, Fell felt as bound to his hate as he was to the Other. The realization was not comforting.

Vengeance is mine, saith the Lord. But Fell had taken it upon himself –and only now had he begun to recoil from what it had done to his humanity, and to his very soul. Yet he knew there was no turning back. What would become of him if he refused the Other that which it craved, and which he had promised?

Day by day, the mountains rose before him. He didn't worry about where he was going; he knew the Other would lead him where he wanted to go. There were mines and claims and mining camps all over, from Canada to the Arizona territory. A lifetime wouldn't have been enough to search them all. So he just kept the kid in his thoughts, and let things take their course.

ix.

Now as the shadows lengthened and the sun sank behind the mountains, Fell sensed that this was it, that the trail ended here. Soon, it'll be over, he told himself. The thought should have cheered him, but he felt nothing, just weariness, and age.

As night fell the sounds from the town grew louder: music jangled discordantly, and there were shouts, voices raised in crude song, the laughter of drunken women. Every so often a gun cracked. Away from the center of town, the clank of pick and shovel went on unabated.

He studied on the situation. The kid would cash in the gold and go on a spree... Fell hoped no one else got to him first. A good strike became everybody's business real quick, and a man with a pocketful of cash was soon another man's mark.

He ate some jerked beef, made some coffee and drank it. When it got good and dark he mounted up and rode toward town. Soon he was passing men on their claims, and could feel their eyes upon him. No doubt every one of them had a gun laid ready to hand, to protect his interests. Fell rode past them silently.

The Other seemed quiet. Perhaps it was only biding its time.

The night's distractions were in full swing as he rode up the main street. In saloons on both sides men were drinking and gambling and talking to the saloon girls. Fell rode slowly, looking in, searching the lamp-lit, flushed faces for one that he knew. Music blared from every door: pianos and music boxes and banjos and raw lusty singing. Out in the street it blended to one horrific roar. Here and there voices boomed out, angry or mirthful; and further up the street a pistol cracked. No one paid it any mind. These men worked hard, and when they got their wages or made a strike, they needed to blow off some steam. None of them cared much what his neighbor did —as long as it didn't interfere with his own pleasures.

At the top of the ridge the street just petered out. Fell dismounted and tied up his horse, then checked the load in his gun. After a moment's reflection, he took a spare gun from the saddlebag, checked it, and stuck it in the small of his back, under his shirt tail.

The first saloon he went into was crowded. There was a faro game in full swing and a scrawny, flat-chested girl was singing to an out of tune player piano but you couldn't make out the song. Men were playing cards at one table and others were drinking at the bar. When he came in a couple of them looked up and shifted uneasily, probably themselves unsure why. Fell looked at them all carefully, one after another: no good. He turned and went back out again.

The next place was a dancehall. The music box was banging, there was a long bar with a mirror along one wall, a French painting on another. The girls might have worked a dozen camps or towns; some of them were probably tougher than most men. When he came in, a couple of them looked him over and started his way, then hesitated. Fell went to the bar and ordered a whiskey. He held it in his left hand as he turned back to the room. He had to be careful. He knew he could take Sanford in a fair fight, but the kid would shoot him in the back if he saw Fell first.

This was the kid's kind of place, he knew that. He loved whores better than anything else except getting drunk. But the kid wasn't there. Fell looked carefully into every man's face, to no avail. And now one of the girls had overcome her apprehensions and was approaching him, smiling.

"Howdy, stranger," she said. "Haven't seen you before. Buy a girl a drink?"

He looked into her eyes, searchingly. He trusted no one; but what if she knew something?

"Okay," he said. "Tell the bartender what you want."

"Thank you very kindly," she said. But she didn't have to say anything; the bartender just brought her a whiskey.

Fell kept watching the room but he could feel her studying him. The scars, he thought. I ain't a very pretty sight. She's probably trying to get her courage up.

He glanced down, saw she'd finished her drink. He drank off his, called the bartender and pointed to the glasses.

"Well, I'm much obliged," she said, a smile on her face. "I see you're a gentleman –you know how to treat a lady."

He grinned a little at that and sipped some of the whiskey, all the time watching the door and the room. There was a stairway, too, in the back, probably to the girls' cribs.

"Are you new in town, mister..." she said.

He ignored her question. Inside him, the Other stirred; he didn't know why.

"I only ask because I haven't seen you before, and I know I would remember," she went on.

He glanced at her. Something about her eyes was like a cat's, frank but closed, distant.

"Yep," he said. "Just got in today."

"There! I knew it," she said. "And you came to the best place in town. We'll make you right at home."

He didn't answer. She threw back her whiskey, a little drunk now.

"You know," she said, "you don't look like a miner... Oh, but I don't mean nothing, it takes all kinds. I'm sure you'll make a strike."

"I didn't come here to mine," he said.

"Are you an outlaw, then?" she said, her voice low.

"No," he said. "Just looking for somebody." Once he'd said it, he wished he hadn't. But she only said, "Oh, I see," looking at her empty drink.

He bought her another and made up his mind. "Maybe you've seen my friend," he said. "Young feller. Red hair, clean shaven." He paused, watching her reaction. "Goes by the name of Sanford."

She shook her head. "Doesn't say much to me," she said. "Of course, a place like this... We see a lot of fellers. You just can't remember 'em all."

He nodded and put down his glass; but when he glanced at her face again it was gone. A skull leered at him, framed by her curled blond hair. The weird went through him like a shot. The room reeled, turning blood-red; and the music, suddenly discordant, jangled in his ears. The skull continued to grin at him even as one hand played with the necklace that lay on her bosom. Words came from its mouth in her voice, but he couldn't make them out.

It was too much –he had to get out of there. He turned and dropped coins on the bar, pushed past the girl and stumbled out the door.

It was cooler outside and the weird faded a little. He took off his hat and passed a hand over his head. His hair was damp with sweat.

Two miners went past. They looked at him curiously, but went on into the dancehall. He made himself get moving. The last thing he needed was to get noticed, make people suspicious. He walked back to his horse and patted her on the flank. She rolled her eyes at him and swished her tail. It struck him that she was the only creature on earth who cared for him.

Standing there under the stars, he wished he were someplace else –someplace there were trees, and cool water, the busy activity of little birds. Someplace like home. Why hadn't he gone back, when the War was over? Most men had. Sure, things were bad there, but even in '65 the worst was done, and it was time to rebuild.

Men had rebuilt the South, but he'd just drifted. The War had changed him, and somehow he'd been reluctant or afraid to change back, to even try to change back. Now he saw that he'd made a wreck of his life. Regret bit into his heart, but it was too late. Overhead the stars swam in the vast sky. They seemed to be laughing at him.

He took the reins in his hand, thinking to ride out – but to where? You can't ride off and leave yourself behind. He'd come here to settle a score. That wasn't much when it came to giving a man's life meaning, but it was better than nothing.

He patted the mare on the neck and started down the street again. He stopped in every saloon, studied every face, drank one glass after another of the cheap raw whiskey as he watched men come and go, and listened to their talk.

Mining towns are small towns, and most don't last all that long. For the most part everyone knows everyone. There are only the miners and those who have come to cater to their needs or despoil them, if not both. And word of a good strike goes around –fast. If the kid had come here with the old man's gold, and was spending any of it, people would know, and be talking about it. But he heard nothing. Maybe he was wrong, and the kid wasn't here? Or maybe when he was around, people just weren't talking.

He saw their looks, the expressions on their faces. He inspired fear in some, a sort of loathing or disgust in others. Even fearless or bellicose men seemed ill at ease in his presence, as if touched by something they could not understand. The scars on his face weren't pretty, that was certain, but he knew this was something more, something they sensed and instinctively shunned.

The night wore on, the saloons thinning out. There were a couple of fistfights, and every so often the report of a gun; drunks staggered home to sleep it off, and men who had lost at cards stalked away, anger and despair on their faces; and there were others, sober and watchful, who waited in the shadows, seeking their prey. Only the uglier girls were left, strident and hoarse, trying desperately to snare a man –but even these, unless sodden with drink, shied clear of Fell. And still no sign of the kid.

He'd come almost to the end of town. From here you could see the claims stretching away into the dark. He went into the last saloon on the street, but they were already sweeping up, the place empty. The barkeep's bleary eyes turned to him and his eyebrows jumped. "Closing time," he said.

Fell nodded. Why not take a chance? He said, "Looking for somebody."

The barkeep was already shaking his head, but Fell went on: "Have you seen a young feller, red-haired, clean shaven? He might be spending pretty freely."

"Ain't seen nobody," the man said. "Closing time. You get on out."

Fell nodded and left again. Inside him, the Other stirred. Why had it led him here? Did it simply hunger? Or was there something more?

He hesitated, unsure what to do. He'd been from one end of town to another and found nothing. And it was late. He turned back, thinking to get his horse and ride out, find someplace to camp for the night. He'd try again the next day, comb through the damned place until he was sure.

There was raucous laughter ahead. For a moment he paid it no mind, occupied with his thoughts. But a saloon door banged open in front of him and a man fell into the street. He sprawled in the dirt. Rage was written on his face and his hand went for his gun. A pistol cracked, twice, and he fell back, dark stains blooming on his shirt.

Fell stopped where he was, watching from the darkness. Another man stepped out of the saloon, still laughing, and crouched down by the body. He went through the dead man's pockets, examining one thing after another, throwing most aside. One or two he put in his own pocket. A second man came out and leaned against a post as he rolled a cigarette. "What you doing, Jimmy?" he said lazily. "You done took all his money."

"Never know," the one called Jimmy said. "I found me a gold watch." As he turned to address the other man, Fell started in surprise: the two looked exactly alike.

Twins: the old prospector had said two of his assailants were just alike. Mean sons of bitches. He felt his chest go tight but stayed just where he was, scarcely even breathing.

The one standing up lit his cigarette and said, "As if you needed to know the time. Why'nt you take his boots while you're at it? Them are pretty nice boots."

Jimmy looked, pulled a boot off the dead man's foot and held it to his own. "Nope," he said. "Too small."

A burst of women's laughter came from inside the saloon. The other man glanced back and said, "Well, if you're 'bout done, them two whores are waitin' on us. Course, if you're not interested any more, I can take your'n, too."

"The hell you say, Johnny," Jimmy said, getting up and dusting off his hands. "She's mine, all mine." He slapped the other on the back and they went back in the saloon, laughing.

Fell let out his breath slowly. Jimmy and Johnny... as alike as two peas in a pod. It had to be them. But where was the kid?

He stood there a minute, studying on it. It was useless to follow them inside. All the saloons were closing, and the twins would be holed up with their girls the rest of the night. But tomorrow... He'd tail them tomorrow. Sooner or later, they'd lead him to the kid.

x.

He walked back to his horse along the almost-empty street, mounted up and rode back out of town the way he'd come. A couple miles back, past the claims and mines, was a little stream near a stand of cottonwood. He made camp there.

When it got light he made coffee, mounted up and rode back into town. The miners were already at work, the pick- and shovel-falls ringing through the clear morning air. Fell was in no hurry; he figured the twins would lay a-bed with their girls half the morning. When he passed the saloon, his hat pulled low over his eyes, it was still closed. He stopped at the livery stable and left his horse, and went on to the hotel, a decent-sized place on the cross street. He took a room, left his saddlebags and rifle, but stuck his extra gun in the small of his back.

It was after nine. He walked back to the saloon, staying in the shadows and avoiding the eyes of others. The place was just opening up. He loitered across the street, a little ways down, surveying the situation.

The barkeep stepped through the door, sweeping. He looked straight at Fell, his expression so blank and void of interest that he might have been thinking anything. Fell scratched the back of his neck, looking down and away, then turned and went along to the general mercantile. He bought the best cigar they had, came back out and lit it.

A girl left the saloon and turned his way. Her hair was undone and she looked tired and shopworn in the raw daylight. She hurried past without looking at Fell and went on down the street.

So they were stirring around, getting ready for the day's business. He crossed the street, walking casually, and dawdled in front of a blacksmith's shop. From here he could not be seen from the saloon's upper windows. Jimmy and Johnny had never seen him before, and had no reason to think he was interested in them, but they'd robbed and killed for their gold, and might shy at any strangers hanging around.

Nothing happened. Minutes passed; half an hour. Fell smoked his cigar, patient as Job.

A man came out of the saloon and turned the other way. In the glare of the sunlight, Fell couldn't tell if it was one of them or not. He hesitated, unsure whether to follow. But now a second man came out, turning his way: one of the twins. Jimmy or Johnny? It didn't matter.

The man walked straight toward him, looking tired and irritable, his eyes bloodshot. Fell waited, the cigar between his teeth. The weird came on him, strong. The street yawed sickeningly, then righted, blood-red. Fell saw the skull beneath the other man's skin, the bony clutch of skeleton hands on his gunbelt. Spurs clattered on the boardwalk like a rattler.

"Jimmy," Fell said lowly as the other man went by.

Jimmy jumped as if a ghost had spoken. He turned, ashamed and angry. "Who are you?" he demanded.

"Name's Fell," he said, alert for his reaction.

There wasn't any. "So?" Jimmy said. "What do you want? How'd you know my name?"

"Everybody knows who you are." Fell's gaze bored into the other man's. "You're a bad hombre. But I'm just lookin' for somebody."

"Who's that?" Fell could see that Jimmy was jumpy, very jumpy. He drew on the cigar, blew out smoke.

"The one who was with you when you got all that gold. You remember, Jimmy. When you killed that old prospector back down in the canyons."

"Why, you son of a..." He went for his gun but it never cleared leather, and the curse died with him. Fell looked down at his gun, and at Jimmy's shirt drenched in blood. The Other, exultant and laughing, went to take Jimmy's soul.

Folks came out on the street up and down the block. They looked at Jimmy, they looked at Fell, and most of them went straight back inside. One or two exchanged words lowly. A man from the saloon stared for a long moment, turned and went up the street.

Fell looked around at them all as he reloaded and holstered the gun. He too turned up the street, walking slowly. He wanted them to see him, wanted word to get around. Killing Jimmy would bring Johnny, and then... Whatever happened should flush out the kid.

At the cross street he went over to the hotel and sat down in one of the chairs on the porch. His mouth was dry and he would have liked a drink, but things might start to happen pretty quick now. The Other was back again, eager, its blood lust like a wire pulled taut. Fell let himself go with it. Why not? Killing Jimmy had given him a little satisfaction. He thought of that canyon, such a lonely place to die, and the old man, bleeding to death, next to the horse he'd loved, shot before his worn-out eyes. He thought of the stolen strike, the nuggets of gold, extracted so painfully, with such labor, from the clutch of the rock, to be thrown away so carelessly on cheap liquor and cheap girls and pointless games of chance. Fell didn't give a damn about his fellow man, but one less Jimmy made the world a mite better.

The air was warm and dry; the day was going to be hot. Fell took off his hat and wiped his brow, then re-lit the stub of the cigar. The Other stirred, avid and voracious.

A group of men went by on the main street, headed toward the saloon. Fell was pretty sure one of them was Johnny. He'd be back.

It didn't take long. In five minutes or less Johnny came around the corner, headed straight for him. He had his hands on his gunbelt and you could see the rage in his livid face. Fell stood up and threw the cigar away. Inside him, the Other tensed, sensing blood. Johnny came to a stop. Fell stepped down off the porch and faced him.

"You the one who killed my brother?" Johnny demanded. A tic pulled at one corner of his mouth.

"Yep," Fell said.

"You tell me why," Johnny said. Fell didn't answer.

"You tell me why!" His voice was tight.

"For the same reason," Fell said, "that I'm gonna kill you."

Johnny's face twitched but he laughed, a short bark of a laugh. "You want to tell me what that is?"

"Why not?" Fell said. "I told Jimmy." The street had turned crimson, and now Fell was looking into the face of a corpse. The grave had left it pale and the skin was rotting away in strips, exposing the cheekbones and jaw and teeth.

"It's the gold, Johnny," Fell said. "I found that old man you robbed, back down in the canyons. He lived long enough to tell me what you done –how you robbed him and killed his horse, then gut-shot him and left him to die. That's why I killed Jimmy. Now it's your turn."

Johnny spit in disdain –then went for his gun. He was quick, but Fell's gun leapt into his hand. The Other laughed as Fell fired three times. The bullets caught Johnny, spun him around, and dropped him in the dust. With a rush, the Other went to feed.

He heard a noise behind him like a hammer cocking back, and a hateful, familiar voice said, "Abraham Fell."

Fell didn't move, just looked at Johnny lying in the dust, red blossoms of blood staining his shirt. But the kid laughed, that mocking laugh that Fell hated so.

"Abraham Fell!" the kid said, and laughed again. "Goddamn, old man! I done left you for dead once, and here you are back. Well, you just drop that ol' six-shooter on the ground, and then turn around, so I can get a look at you."

Fell dropped his gun and turned around. The kid was holding a double-barreled shotgun on him. He looked older now, a little more trail worn –but he had the same head of red hair that would never comb, the same insolent cunning in his eyes. A grin split his face.

"Whoo-ee, look at you. Well, I may not have killed you, old man, but I sure didn't leave you lookin' any prettier, either. Should have done the job right the first time."

"Would have been better for you if you had."

The kid laughed again. He had the shotgun aimed right at Fell's midsection. "Ain't that a fine way to greet an old friend," he said, and went on: "Cause I know you been looking for me. My girl told me, last night. You know, at first I couldn't imagine who it was, when she told me an ugly old man with scars on his face and just one eye was asking about me. I just couldn't figure it. You know, you just don't expect a man to come back from the dead."

"No," Fell said, watching the gun.

"Fact is," the kid said, "I still didn't get it till I seen you. You should be dead, old man! Why ain't you dead?"

"Indians found me."

"Injuns," the kid said with contempt. "Well, it's my own fault. I let that Pinkie spook me."

"Pinkie," Fell said. "I seen him a while back."

"He can go to Hell."

"He's waiting for you there." Fell's hand went slowly to his shirt pocket and took out Pinkie's ring. He tossed it to the kid, who caught it out of the air and looked at it, scowling. But the shotgun was still on Fell's middle.

After a moment the kid threw the ring in the dirt. "Pinkie was yellow. He had the nerves of a girl."

"Nice way to talk about a friend."

"Friends are for losers," the kid spat. Fell looked at him, thinking of Max, letting the contempt show on his face. The kid pointed to Johnny's body. "You prob'ly think you done something there, something big. Well, them two weren't no friends of mine. I got no friends. They was business associates, that's all. Now that they're dead, their part belongs to me." He laughed again. "That's all you done, Fell. You done give their share to me."

The sun was hot, beating down. Fell took off his hat and ran his hand over his hair. "You know, Sanford," he said, "I came to kill you on account of Max, of what you done to Max. But if I hadn't sworn to do it I'd be tempted to let you live, 'cause you're already in Hell. Wherever you go, you got your own little Hell, right there inside you."

The Other slid back down inside him, tense and eager.

"You stupid old man," the kid exploded. "Nobody's gonna kill me. I'm gonna cut you in half, and when I'm done they'll pin a badge on me and make me marshal of this town."

The weird came over Fell now, strong. The kid went on talking but his voice was drowned by a clank of picks and shovels, digging graves. A crow flew up and landed on the rail of the hotel's porch. It fixed Fell with one bright eye and stared, unblinking. Fell couldn't look away from it; the bird seemed to subjugate his will. In its eye he saw a series of Hells, each one full of souls in torment, and worse than the last; and he knew that his place was there.

The shotgun roared and he felt himself jerked back – back to the street near the hotel, where the kid had fired into the air and was shouting at him in a rage. But now the kid had a noose around his neck and his face was black, his tongue protruding even as he shouted, and Fell could scarcely make out the words: "...damned old man... pay attention when I'm talking... gettin' senile? ...out in the sun too long... gone soft in the head..." The crow, too, was cawing, louder and louder, over and over again. Fell looked around and saw dozens, hundreds of them, perched on every roof and cawing their heads off.

"Shut up!" the kid screamed, and swung the shotgun toward the one on the porch. He pulled the trigger and the shotgun jumped, roaring –but the crow lifted off, cawing hoarsely. A window shattered, glass smashing to the ground.

The street see-sawed and everything went back to normal. There was the most perfect silence. The kid looked down at the shotgun and threw it aside. He turned squarely toward Fell. Glaring insanely, he went for his gun.

Fell dropped to one knee as he pulled the spare gun from the small of his back. Surprise crossed the kid's face and then Fell was pulling the trigger. The shots took the kid in the chest and stomach, throwing him back. His dying fingers squeezed off a shot that smacked into the façade of the hotel. He landed flat on his back and lay still. The Other sprang for its prey, laughing. Fell heard the crow cawing again. He looked up: it was perched on the roof of the hotel, its raucous cries ringing through the streets. It paused long enough to look down and fix his gaze with one knowing eye.

Fell holstered his gun, listening. A mutter of voices had begun: folks guessed the shooting was over and were emerging from where they'd hunkered down. He picked up his other gun, dusted it off, and reloaded, wondering if there'd be trouble. He waited, staring vacantly at the bodies, listening to the crow and feeling nothing.

No one approached him. A few stood in the shadows, looking, as others moved on, going back to their business. Maybe the men he'd killed hadn't been very well liked. But they weren't going to thank him, either.

He walked closer to the kid and stood looking down. He thought that he wanted to remember. The kid's skin was ashen, and instead of his mocking expression, a look of fear and pain was fixed on his face. It was over. It had taken so long, he'd come so far, and now it was over.

The Other

The crow fell silent. Fell looked up. The bird looked him in the eye once more, then lifted off and flew away.

xi.

He walked back to the main street and went into the first saloon he saw. Voices were raised in excited talk but as soon as he came in they stopped and men began to quietly leave. The barkeep came over, a sullen look on his face. Fell pointed: "How much for the bottle?"

"Two bucks."

He paid and left with it. Near the hotel, a small group was gathered, looking at the kid's body, but when they saw him coming, most moved on. He went past into the hotel and up to his room.

While he was drinking the Other came back, replete and satisfied. Fell pretended not to notice.

Had he laid Max's ghost? He didn't know, and he couldn't even get drunk. When the bottle was empty, he lay down on the bed and looked up at the ceiling. He should have been happy, or anyway, satisfied –but he felt nothing, not even relief that it was finally all over. Over –but that was a laugh. There was still the Other, to whom he was bound, a demonic Siamese twin.

All that afternoon he lay there, wishing he could feel, and feeling nothing. Dusk came, then dark, the town gearing up for the night's pleasures, music grinding, voices hooting and grunting and yelping, and every now and then the crack of a gun. He thought of the gold the kid had taken from the old man: who'd spend it now? Whoever found it, he guessed. It hardly mattered anymore. Nothing did.

Max was almost lost to him now: he couldn't recall his face, or the sound of his voice. The kid was the same, though only that morning he'd shot him dead; and the others were still less real, spectral, nearly forgotten. He looked down at his hands, old now, weather-beaten and lined. Would it be so bad if he, too, passed on, and was forgotten?

He went to the window. The brutish merry-making was unbearable; he longed to make it stop. He picked up the gunbelt, took his gun from its holster. The feel and weight of it were comforting. One shot...

Watchful, the Other gathered itself in anticipation. And he understood: it would take his soul just as it had taken the souls of all the others he had killed. He holstered the gun. "No," he said out loud, though no one else was there. "You're not getting mine yet, you bastard."

Was it he or the Other who laughed now? He didn't know. He stretched back out on the bed. Tomorrow he'd ride out. It didn't much matter where.

Automata

23 June 1871

Found Juanita this morning, the Mexican girl who helped with the cooking and cleaning. How she came to be in the workshop is impossible to say; curiosity, perhaps. Idle curiosity is a vice that seldom goes unpunished. She'd been warned to stay out of there; she should have listened. As it was, found her battered and broken on the workshop floor, her blood in great pools and gouts, and the creation spattered and smeared with it.

Not its fault. Clearly, it had functioned perfectly, even admirably; but it had no idea of its partner's *fragility*.

25 June 1871

Had to cremate the girl's body, along with her effects. Some trouble when her relatives came looking for her. Apparently a proper suitor has approached them with a very advantageous offer. They must have stood to come by a tidy sum. Would not accept the explanation that she'd eloped with a *vaquero* she met in town. According to them, she wasn't like that. They all repeated as much, but the father was the worst. He reeked of tequila, flared up when told she wasn't there, questioned everything, muttered vague threats.

7 July 1871

For days Juanita's father has been coming back. Found him snooping around just this morning. Finally the shotgun convinced him to go. The avaricious peasant cursed me and swore he'd return. The man is a nuisance and worse, a menace. If he comes back again he will have to be eliminated.

31 July 1871

Since last, there have been others, unfortunately. The creation's appetites are quite human, and once whetted... Tried to explain, in a non-Christian framework, about control of the desires. The creation appeared to understand; not sure if in fact it did. But in sum, I have succeeded, beyond what I'd even dared hope. One has to expect some minor difficulties.

From the journal of Ernst Ludvig Kuhn, Baron von Steiner

*   *   *

She drove south out of town in the rented wagon, tired and apprehensive, her heart heavier than ever. When she'd gotten off the train that morning, she thought she was glad to arrive, at least. Four days by rail –four days of the cramped car, of dust and cinders and steam –after that a person would be glad to arrive anywhere. But the empty platform reminded her that no one waited for her there; no one even knew she was coming. The deep sadness of her purpose washed through her once again; but maybe, she told herself, maybe this would lay it all to rest for good. At least she'd see the grave.

Morning, but the sun was already hot. She picked up her valise and walked into the relative darkness of the depot, on through and out the other side. Before her, and stretching away into the same hot sunlight, was the dusty main street of the town.

A number of people were out, going about their business. They were a bit rough-looking –miners for the most part, she guessed, and good-time girls all dolled-up but looking hard around the eyes and mouth –but she supposed she'd be safe enough. She went to the livery stable first, to rent a buckboard and horse. The hostler was a taciturn man, so she kept it brief, and paid in advance. When she asked where she'd find the marshal, he just pointed.

Wanted posters hung outside the marshal's office, and when she went in she found him cleaning a rifle. He stood up when he saw her, a tall man, well-built, with a weather-tanned face and hands and a certain frankness in his eyes. She held out a hand.

"Marshal, I'm Sarah Hayworth. You don't know me, but you may well have known my father."

His eyes narrowed. "Sarah *Hayworth*? Then you're Frank Hayworth's daughter?"

"That's right."

"Well, pleased to meet you, ma'am. Have a seat, please, there's no need to stand. I'm sure you've come a long ways?"

"Thank you. I arrived this morning from Memphis."

She sat down across from him. He put the rifle aside and studied her.

"Memphis is a long ways from here, Miss Hayworth. I reckon you've come..."

"To settle my father's estate."

"Right. Well, as you may know, he's buried out at his place. Seems that's how he wanted it. Course, if you want the body, ah, exhumed, so's to take it back with you, I'm sure we can arrange to get you some help."

"Thank you." She looked down at the desk, troubled: at the word 'exhumed', she'd felt the wound open in her heart again. "I... I haven't yet made up my mind."

"Of course... Well, tell me: what can I do for you?"

She shifted in place, pulling herself together. "Yes, well, I came to you as I don't know anyone in town. I thought perhaps you could tell me how to get to his place."

"Sure thing." He took a piece of paper and drew a map. "I'd take you myself but my deputy's gone and I have to mind the store. But anyone could drive you..."

"That's alright, I've hired a wagon." She stood up and he did the same. "Will you be stopping at the hotel?" he asked.

"No, I think I'll stay at Dad's place."

He nodded, looking awkward. She waited, and after a moment he said, "Miss Hayworth, have you... Have you come here alone?"

"Yes," she answered. She was going to leave it at that but he frowned and she went on: "My mother died years ago. There were no other children. I was married but my husband was killed in a riverboat accident. After his death, I went back to my maiden name." She paused, and added: "So you see, there was no one else."

"Yes, of course." He had a serious air about him, and she thought he wanted to say something else, but all he said was: "My condolences, Miss Hayworth. If I can be of service to you, please let me know."

Now, driving south out of town, it struck her how truly alone she was. The road ahead, little more than two ruts, was as empty as the country; and though the mountains loomed nearby, their high peaks covered in snow, the sky was somehow huge. This vastness impressed her, but though beautiful, it seemed remote, aloof. Somehow, the very fact of explaining her situation to the marshal had brought sharply home her complete isolation. True, she'd lost her parents, and she had no close relations, but in Memphis she was part of things, she knew people. Here, she knew no one; almost no one was even aware she existed. As she thought through that, a certain anxiety grew within her, and she wondered if she'd been wise to come. But what choice had there been? There was no one else. No: the responsibility was hers, and she would have to rely upon herself. That, after all, was what her father had always tried to instill in her.

She thought of him as he'd been when she was growing up. He'd always tried so hard. Without her mother, it hadn't been easy for either of them. As a girl, she'd wondered why he never remarried. Now she suspected he'd loved her mother too much for that, and had poured what he could of his bereaved love into their child. What he did with the rest, she couldn't say. But he'd insisted on her getting a good education. "Sarah," he'd say, "an education makes all the difference in this world. With an education, you make your own way. You don't have to depend on anyone else."

And he'd been right: what she'd made as a teacher had always been sufficient for her needs. Even at the lowest periods of her life, it hadn't been with money problems that she had struggled. As for her father... well, he'd gone his own way, too. He'd had a good education, in the east, but the professions had never interested him; and after quarreling with his own father over the choice of a career, he left the family home, never to return. He served in the military for a time, dabbled in mining, engineering, timber, mining again... She wasn't sure what all. But once he'd seen her set up in life, he headed west, driven by motives obscure even to himself. His infrequent letters explained little, but she believed he'd struggled for a long time. Then came the strike he'd waited for: a silver lode, high grade and plentiful. He'd finally done it: he was a rich man, a self-made man. She'd been so happy for him —not so much for the money, but to know his dreams had finally come true. He'd asked her to come visit, wrote vaguely of going on to California, buying a ranch. She'd heard nothing more, until that other letter arrived, the one from the lawyer. Her father had been killed in a mining accident, a collapse in the shaft. His estate needed settling.

She recalled the injustice of it, the stunned feeling that God or fate had played them both a bad turn. After the years of hard times, the sacrifices he'd made for her, and the toil and poverty he'd endured, he was dead at the moment of his triumph; and she'd lost him, never to see him again, just as he held out the hope of reuniting.

And now here she was, alone. She supposed that she would be rich now. The idea didn't interest her much, but she wondered what she should do when all the formalities were over: go back to Memphis? Her life was there, such as it was.

Or should she go on to California, buy the ranch he'd wanted, live out his dream for him and in his memory? The idea pleased her, though she knew that California was a young and raw-boned land, and she would have a great deal to learn.

The wagon rattled along. She looked at the marshal's map. Ahead was the stand of cottonwood, with the old adobe hut across the way. She was almost there.

Just past the trees was a lane that went off to the right. She turned the buckboard in there and followed the way, overgrown with rank grass, that led uphill. Here were more trees, and the lane weaved through them, turning, and came out in a cleared space, in front of the house.

She pulled up where the horse could graze, tethered the reins, and climbed down. In the quiet of the afternoon, the wind blew gently. The house was on an eminence, with a nice view to the east. She could imagine her father's pride in it. Though not large, for he'd had little need for extra room, it was stoutly built, with a stone foundation and solid timbers. It stood two storeys high, with heavy shutters for the windows and equally heavy doors. But it had that empty look houses have when no one lives there.

She stood looking at it for a long moment, wondering where the grave was. Back on the road, she'd seen occasional wildflowers. Tomorrow she would gather some to lay there. Probably no one had done that. Funerals were lonely things when your own flesh and blood wasn't there.

She was thinking of what the marshal had said about removing his remains as she walked up the steps to the front door, and so at first she didn't notice the sign. But as she reached the porch she saw it: job-printed like a wanted poster, it read: *WARNING – NO TRESPASSING*. At first she thought confusedly that it had been posted for her own benefit, to warn off others until she should arrive. But in smaller letters, it read: *This real property, and all structures, buildings, outbuildings, etc., pertaining thereto, is in receivership; and as such, is and remains the property of the Northrop Bank.* There followed a legal description of the property, which, however little she was acquainted with the area, corresponded with what she knew of her father's land.

Surprised and rather shocked, she read and re-read the notice several times without being able to understand its import. There must be some mistake, for how came otherwise the bank to claim ownership of her father's home? It had to be a mistake.

She would settle it when she returned to town. There was no hurry. Someone had made a mistake. As soon as she went back to town she would see about it. But right now she was here. This place had belonged to her father and now it came to her, as her inheritance.

As she thought this, she put a hand on the doorknob. It wouldn't open. She rattled it, tried to see if it was stuck. No good: the door was locked.

Even back in Memphis, doors were seldom locked with a key. And who could have *this* key? Who had locked it? Someone from the bank? Somewhat at a loss, she looked about. The windows of the porch were shuttered. Was there perhaps another door?

She heard hoofbeats behind her. Turning, she saw a man on a fine, fast-looking horse. He was well-made and rather handsome, but he had a hard look about him, very hard. She noted the pistol on his hip, the gunbelt full of shells, a rifle in its scabbard on the horse. He did not smile as he touched the brim of his hat.

"Howdy, ma'am," he said. His tone was polite but not friendly. "May I help you?"

"Good afternoon," she said. "I don't know if you can. I need the key to this door."

"I wouldn't have that, ma'am," he said. "Besides, as you can plainly see, the place is posted, no trespassing."

The words were not calculated to please. She drew herself up, raising her chin; but it struck her that he had no way of knowing who she was.

"This place belonged to my father," she said evenly. "After his death, I inherited it. It belongs to me now."

"I don't know what you're talking about," the man said coldly. "This here place belongs to the Northrop Bank, and it's the bank that hired me to keep an eye on it. If you want to take issue with that, you'll have to do so with the bank. For now," he added, his eyes narrowing, "I think you'd best be on your way."

She stared at him, shocked and angry; and he returned her gaze coolly, his expression disdainful. She wondered what he might do, how he might back up his order to leave, but decided it would be best not to find out.

"Very well," she said. "I'd have you know, sir, that thanks to your reception, I've not even had the opportunity to lay eyes on my father's grave. But I shall indeed address myself to the bank, to 'take issue' with the situation, as you have it, and then I shall return to claim my rightful property."

She strode down the steps and past him to the buckboard. He watched her, saying nothing, as she turned around and headed back down the lane, toward town.

*   *   *

At the bank she waited three-quarters of an hour before Mr. Northrop could see her. She spent the time watching the comings and goings and telling herself to keep her composure. She'd driven back angry, very angry, but now she presented the most perfect calm, determined to sound out the situation first, ahead of anything else.

Northrop was a stout man, not tall, with thinning hair and a florid complexion. He wore an Eastern suit with a heavy gold watch chain drawn over the vest and a pair of tooled leather boots. Ushering her into his office with a great show of courtesy, he apologized for the wait, and had her sit down on an upholstered chair facing his desk. As she explained her business, his face guarded an almost mask-like expression of concern and deference. She suspected his true thoughts were otherwise, so she kept her account short and neutral in tone, and awaited his explanation. He sighed first, blew his nose in a silk handkerchief –he seemed to have some difficulty breathing –and said in a conciliatory tone, "Firstly, Miss Hayworth, please accept my condolences on the death of your father. He was a fine man."

Lowering her eyes, she nodded, then looked at him evenly.

"Moreover," he went on, "I sincerely regret the reception you found at your father's home. The man to whom you refer is indeed in the employ of the bank. He is responsible for protecting the property, and obviously had no idea to whom he was speaking. Please accept my most sincere apologies for the rudeness with which you were treated."

"That's alright," she said. "He was only doing his job. There was no way for him to know..."

"Well, that's exactly right," Northrop exclaimed, and blew his nose again. "None of us knew you were coming. Why, if I'd known... I'd have driven you there and opened the place up myself. In fact I'd do so right now except I have another appointment. But you'll have the key; you'll take it with you when you go. It's natural to want to see the place..."

"And my father's grave," Sarah said. "Your man stopped me before I could visit it."

"A misunderstanding." He blew his nose again. "A terrible misunderstanding. It won't happen again. I know you'll want to have some of his things. Take whatever you like."

"I plan to, Mr. Northrop." She was afraid she sounded less pleasant than she wanted. "In point of fact, as my father's heir, I don't see that I need your –or anyone's –permission."

"Ah!" he said, his face bright red. "No –of course not. At least not in what concerns his personal possessions."

"And the real property, Mr. Northrop?" The air was suddenly very tense. She watched his eyes, which shifted about, avoiding hers. "Can you explain to me why it's posted on the door that the real property now belongs to the bank?"

"Well, as to that, Miss Hayworth..."

"Yes?" She did not suppress the insistence in her voice.

"Well, you see, your father had debts... Upon his death, the bank naturally looked to recover its interests."

"Debts?" she said sharply. "It was my understanding he'd made an excellent strike in silver."

"Yes, but, you see... There'd been reverses..."

"Reverses? Excuse me, Mr. Northrop, but you are not talking to just anyone. I happen to be my father's sole heir. Now will you kindly explain a little more clearly?"

He stood up with a sigh and went to a cabinet on one side of the room. From it he withdrew a file and returned to his desk, opened it and put on a pair of glasses. Standing up, lips pursed, he turned over page after page in the file, going through it all, and then closed it again and put the glasses away. His expression had something regretful about it. Though impatient with this performance, she waited. At length, as if forced unwillingly to a duty he found distasteful, he said, "Indeed, you are correct, Miss Hayworth: your father struck a sizeable vein of silver, and overnight became a very rich man.

"However, serious losses in recent times all but reversed that situation. Finding himself in dire need of working capital, he came to me. The bank made loans in excess of one hundred thousand dollars, collateral for which was provided by the mine itself and other real property owned by your father. Unfortunately, not a cent of those loans has ever been repaid. Therefore, upon your father's death, the bank filed a petition to foreclose on the property."

"You work pretty fast out here."

The banker looked mildly offended. "Miss Hayworth, the due period of sixty days was strictly observed."

"Which didn't allow me much time to get here."

"Your father died intestate. Mention of you was found among his papers. His attorney wrote you at your last known address."

"It seems to me you have a very plausible answer for everything, Mr. Northrop, but the curious fact remains that I had every reason to believe my father a wealthy man, yet I arrive here to find that he died ruined and penniless." She paused, watching him carefully. "Now can you tell me this: what caused these 'reverses', as you have it, in my father's fortune?"

The banker put on such an air now that one might have taken him for the undertaker. "Ah, Miss Hayworth... This is difficult for me. I'm afraid the answer may be rather painful for you."

"I am prepared to hear what you have to say."

"Indeed... Ah, but, human nature, you know... Man is so prone to weakness..."

"Mr. Northrop, are you the parson or the banker?"

A shadow of annoyance crossed his face and was gone.

"Very well, Miss Hayworth, it amounts to this: your father grew addicted to gambling. It became a passion with him, a fatal passion, and more. And you see, a mining town draws the sort of person who will prey upon others in search of easy money: unscrupulous persons, professional gamblers, and the like. Your father ended by losing everything he had."

A long pause followed his words. At length, she said, "Mr. Northrop, you mean to tell me my father lost one hundred thousand dollars... by *gambling*?"

"That much, and more. One hundred thousand represents only the amount loaned to him by the bank."

She took a moment to turn this over in her mind. "May I examine the documents in the file?"

"But of course." He tendered her the papers. She went through them one by one, carefully, then returned the file, and stood up.

"Very well, Mr. Northrop. I believe you promised me the key to my father's home?"

"Yes, yes, of course." He took the key from a drawer and gave it to her.

"Thank you very much. I shall be in contact with you again."

He hurried from behind his desk to open the door for her. She acknowledged his courtesy with a nod, and left.

*   *   *

Squinting in the brilliant sun, she crossed the street and went up to the marshal's office. The marshal was studying some papers when she came in. He nodded to her. "Find your father's place alright, Miss Haywood?"

"Yes, marshal, thank you."

"Everything okay up there?"

"Well, I suppose." She wondered how far to trust him, decided not too far at first. "In fact, it's locked up tight. I had to get the key from Mr. Northrop, at the bank. And now, according to documents he showed me, it seems that the bank owns the property."

The marshal was not surprised. He nodded: "Yep. I could've told you that, but I figured you'd best find out on your own."

She studied him. He looked slightly uncomfortable, as if something weighed on his mind. She didn't know what she stood to gain, but she said, "Marshal, I heard tell that my father gambled all his money away."

He nodded. "Yep. That's what I heard tell, too."

"A hundred thousand dollars –*more* than a hundred thousand dollars –is a lot to lose at cards."

"It sure is," he agreed glumly. "I guess sometimes a fellow just gets on a roll –carried away –and don't know when to stop. Or maybe he *can't* stop."

"Yes." This wasn't getting anywhere, and she could see he wasn't going to tell her anything. "Well," she said firmly, "I think I need to see my father's attorney. Can you tell me where to find him?"

He gave her the name and address and she left. Climbing into the buckboard, she could see that someone watched her from the bank's window. She paid it no mind and drove away.

The attorney's office was on the second floor of a building that also housed a dry-goods store and a barber shop. She tied up and went up the stairs, to a narrow hallway, rather dim, with a row of doors. Painted on the frosted glass of one was: *J.P. Martinson, Attorney at Law – Notary Public.* She knocked and a voice called out to come in.

Mr. Martinson, Esq., was an old man, bleary-eyed, with only a few strands of hair carefully combed across his bald scalp. He stood up when he saw her: stooped, so thin his clothes hung on him baggily, he looked quite unwell, yet he had a definite keenness in his expression and his glance. His hand tried absently to brush away the snuff stains on his vest. She introduced herself.

"Ah, yes, Miss Hayworth –do sit down." He gestured toward a horsehair seat facing his desk. "This is a pleasure, even if the circumstances are unhappy. I thought a great deal of your father."

His voice was alternately grating and tremulous but he struck her as kind and even rather prepossessed in her favor. He spoke pleasantly of her father, with whom he had apparently done a fair amount of business without, perhaps, knowing him too intimately; but she was hardly surprised, for her father had been a very private man, and solitary in his habits. Martinson had been in the town a long time, and seemed to be largely familiar with its inhabitants. She watched his hands shake as he took out a silver snuff box and take a snort, and wondered, a little sadly, how long he had to live. Mortality, it seemed, had become a common theme of her thoughts. But the old man had brought the conversation around to her business.

He listened, attentive but impassive, to her account: her understanding of the state of her father's affairs; the news of his death; her arrival, visit with the marshal, and trip to the home; and her meeting with the banker. Now and then he nodded in confirmation, or to indicate he understood; occasionally he put the tips of his fingers together, and looked past them into space; as she spoke of Northrop, he frowned slightly. But he said nothing until she finished, and then said only, "I see." And then he seemed to wait. She felt unaccountably hopeless as she went on: "Mr. Martinson, you knew my father. Does Mr. Northrop's account seem plausible?"

"How do you mean?" he answered.

"Why," she said, "so much about it... There just seems something wrong about it all. The very idea of him gambling is absurd: he never gambled. He looked down on gambling, and was scornful of those who did so. He called it foolish, and a waste of hard-earned money. I've never even known him to play cards, not even once."

"People change," observed the lawyer.

"Do they change that much? Enough to lose a fortune? No: mining was the sort of gamble that appealed to my father.

Something solid, where knowledge and training are at play, not a game of cards. But in the documents, there was no indication of *business* losses... Nothing with any records at all."

"Excuse me?"

"You understand what I'm saying, Mr. Martinson: if a man has losses in business, there are records –receipts, bills of sale, documents of some sort. But with cards, there's no records, the money just vanishes into someone's pocket."

Martinson's face was glum. "What are you suggesting, Miss Hayworth?"

She hesitated, unsure of his sympathies, but where else was she to turn? "That it's perhaps a convenient way to account for the disappearance of a man's money –especially if you don't know the man. But the sum involved is so large..."

"That you find it implausible, and thus suspicious."

"Exactly so, Mr. Martinson."

"And yet sums such as that are lost everyday in the gambling halls of Chicago –not to mention on the Exchange."

"But we aren't in Chicago, Mr. Martinson."

"A man can be as big a fool here as anywhere. Or a woman, too," he added.

"Excuse me?"

But he just shook his head, as his palsied hands picked up the snuff box, and set it down again. It was becoming clear to her that this sick old man could not help her –or would not, if he could.

"You are suspicious of what you have been told," he said after a moment, "and rightly so, for it goes against your experience and your better judgment. You say your father never gambled before, that he was opposed to gambling. That may very well be true, but it is also true that what a man does back east and what he does out here are sometimes two very different things. What he is opposed to in some circumstances may seem quite different in others."

"Mr. Martinson," Sarah said, "did you ever know my father to gamble?"

"No," he said firmly. "But I only ever saw him during business hours. We never socialized. Moreover, I do not frequent saloons, gambling houses, dancehalls, or any other sort of establishment where gambling takes place." He coughed, a dry racking cough that seemed to cause him considerable pain. "So you see that my testimony is of no more value than yours."

It was hopeless, she saw that now, but she couldn't just give up.

"Mr. Martinson," she said. "What you say or seem to say is perfectly true: I cannot prove beyond all doubt that my father did not gamble his fortune away. Certainly any notion of plausibility has little value in the courts. But there is something else."

"Yes?" Martinson said.

She gathered herself. "Mr. Northrop permitted me to examine his file. It included several loan documents –the loans on which the bank foreclosed. They were all in good form and duly executed, except for this: on each one of them, my father's signature had been forged."

Martinson started, and a look of something like dread crossed his face. She was afraid she'd gone too far, revealed too much. But he put his fingertips together and composed himself.

"Miss Hayworth, I appreciate your confidence in me, but I sincerely advise you not to repeat that assertion – especially since you are here alone, and essentially unprotected."

She looked at him in surprise. "Mr. Martinson, I'm sure you don't mean to suggest..."

"That to make such a charge is dangerous? I certainly do mean it! Oh, it's alright here... But beyond that door... No, Miss Hayworth: you will surely put your life in danger if you make any such accusation."

"I've accused no one, and of nothing."

"True, and I should keep it that way, for you will have accused a very powerful man of a very serious charge if you make that imputation again."

His shaking hands took a pinch of snuff, spilling half before he could snort it up one nostril. For a time he said nothing more. Frustrated and indignant, she could have railed at the pathetic old man, too frightened to help her or stand up for what was right; but she kept her peace, deeming it best not to judge others, and to rely only upon herself. But she'd had enough, and rose to go. As if against his better judgment, the attorney held up one hand.

"Miss Hayworth, I urge you to reflect on the overall situation. Your father is dead –killed in an accident. Consider that fact objectively, and from a non-emotional standpoint. Nothing can bring him back. His fortune, too, is gone, and there seems little prospect of its recovery. You are unknown here, and alone. The man who controls what remains of your father's estate, and who does so by what you claim are forged documents, this man is powerful and well-known. He has many friends, associates and connections; he is well-esteemed

–and feared. Any claim such as yours would constitute a threat, and not only in the matter which is your particular concern. It would be perceived as a threat to his business interests in general, to his reputation and his fortune –to his life. And I happen to know that any such threat would be treated with the utmost severity and ruthlessness."

She stared at him, shocked. "Really, Mr. Martinson! And you a lawyer! We are discussing a legal matter, one properly settled in court."

"Miss Hayworth, you are not in Memphis. Look down on that street. Every man carries a gun. Why? For protection, to protect his life and interests. I am an attorney at law, it is true, but I know as well as anyone that here in the West, most disputes are settled by violence. That is a simple fact, and no high-minded notion of law or justice will change it. Take my advice, Miss Hayworth: forget about the whole thing. Leave the past alone, and do not stir up trouble that can only bring you grief. Return to Memphis with your father's body and forget about the West."

He would say no more, just turned his sad bleary eyes away. Frustrated and at a loss, she left.

*　　　　　　*　　　　　　*

She thought it over as she drove back to her father's home. She felt tired, put out and discouraged by the meeting, but she couldn't find it in her heart to blame the old man. He was afraid, that was obvious. Was he involved in the whole fraud? It seemed possible, though she doubted it somehow. But he was old and sickly, and such people become cautious. In a way she felt sorry for him.

As for the rest of what he'd said... He'd done little to convince her she was wrong; rather he'd sought to prevent her from making such a charge public. The result was that their meeting tended to confirm her suspicions.

The house and grounds were quiet in the accumulated heat of the day. She tied up in the shade and let herself in with the key, hoping vaguely that the bank's man knew she was to be permitted there. The house was dark and still inside, the air dry and musty. She walked through, opening windows and doors, thinking to air it out.

Though not a spacious home, it was tidy and neat, sparsely furnished in a simple masculine taste. On the ground floor, a front room served as both parlor and study, with a dining room and kitchen behind, and of the three bedrooms upstairs, two were unused and obviously only for guests, who must have been rare. In the bare kitchen she realized with chagrin that in all the confusion she'd neglected to lay in supplies. She'd have to return to town after all.

A bookcase stood against one wall of the front room, near a great roll-top desk that locked with a key. Old and familiar, it had been in their home when she was a child; her father had brought it along when he left Memphis. Seeing it here, dusty and disused, gave her a bitter pang. To some extent, the whole house was like that –the house of a dead man, empty and forlorn. Everything bespoke his absence, and echoed the emptiness in her heart.

Eyes moist, she went out back. Here it was shady, with a smell of juniper in the air. The hill rose precipitately behind the house, blocking the sun, and the air was cooler. She went around the side and found what she was looking for, the small plot that held his grave.

The headstone told his name and the date of his death, nothing more. She looked on it and wondered about the lonely funeral he must have had, in this town where his success was envied and his wealth coveted, where even his friends feared the powers that exercised themselves in avarice and theft. And what was her business here now? He'd made a fortune here and lost it, then lost his life. Had it been worth it? And she'd come now too, and had already been warned off concerning that same fortune.

"Oh, dad," she murmured. But the little plot was a cipher, like all graves, and she turned away no wiser than before.

Back in the house, which was somehow even more desolate than before, she seemed to turn in circles for a time, unsure what to do or where to start. It was getting dark, and she was worn out. She'd planned to stay there but the place had become oppressive, and in any case she had nothing to eat. The obvious answer was to go back to town, put up at the hotel for the night, and return tomorrow.

She closed up, locked the doors, climbed back on the buckboard and set off; and she felt relief as the place fell behind her again. It had been a long and trying day. She would rest, and get a fresh start in the morning.

Hoofbeats pounded behind her. She glanced back, saw five or six men on horseback. They came up at a gallop, passed her on both sides, then cut her off, turning her horse. Frightened, she brought the wagon to a stop amidst loud, rough laughter.

"What is the meaning of this?" she demanded, trying to keep the fear from her voice. "What do you want?"

Several of the men laughed again, unpleasantly. In front of her, a rider reined up. He was a dark man, hard-looking, with a gun on his hip, and cruelty in his wolf-like expression –cruelty, and arrogance. He touched a hand to his hat.

"Begging your pardon, ma'am," he said, in a mockery of courtesy. "But, you see, it's not rightly safe for a lady to be out on the roads at night."

"I thank you for your concern, sir," she said coldly, "but I assure you I have no cause for worry."

Some of the men snickered. She glanced around. They were a rough lot: dirty, unshaven, with hard eyes and faces.

"But that's where you're wrong, ma'am," the first one said. "Right now you've got a great deal of cause for worry."

"You tell her, Blackie!" one of the others shouted, and yipped like a coyote.

Blackie grinned as he swung down from the saddle. He walked easily to the wagon and laid a hand across the reins. She looked at him sharply.

"Oh, not on account of us," he said, grinning. "Why, we're friendly –*real* friendly. Ain't we, boys?" He looked around. The others hooted and jeered: "That's right! –You said it, Blackie! –Real friendly!"

"You see?" Blackie said. "What you have to worry about is folks that are *not* friendly. And there's plenty of 'em. Folks as don't like a woman messing around in their affairs. But as for us..."

He reached out and picked her up by the waist, lifting her out of the wagon, and set her on the ground. She was shocked, and a little afraid. "Now look here..." she began.

"No, *you* look here!" he said. "I just want to show you how friendly we can be." He took her in his arms and kissed her full on the lips. She struggled, but couldn't break his hold. The others all laughed.

When he let her go, she slapped him. He grinned at her but his eyes were cold. He looked around.

"Looks like we got us a bronco here," he said. "May have to fit her with a Spanish bit."

He grabbed her arm, twisting it up behind her back, and slapped the rump of her horse. It broke into a run, the buckboard rattling along behind. Sarah's heart sank.

"I guess you're with us now," Blackie said. "Maybe we'll have us a party."

He kissed her again, roughly. She tried to push him away, then beat at him with her fists, to no avail. When he let her go again, they were all hooting and jeering. She looked him in the eyes as coldly as she could, and spit on the ground. They all laughed again, except for Blackie, whose face colored.

"I see," he said slowly, "that you don't much cotton to friendly folks. Maybe you think you're a little too good for us. Well, we can fix that."

He slapped her across the face with his open hand – she saw stars –threw her to the ground and stood over her, hand ready to strike again. "Let's see you without them city clothes. I bet you're just like any old saloon gal, then."

Face numbed by the blow, she looked away, sickened by his brutality, and shocked at what was happening. He was reaching for her blouse when a rifle cracked. The bullet just missed Blackie, ricocheted off rock and zinged away.

The horsemen pulled their guns, looking about in all directions, baffled. One of them, a youngish thug with a wispy beard, gave a shout and fired into the dark. Instantly the rifle cracked again and he gasped as a bullet slammed into his shoulder. The gun fell from his fingers; bending over the horse's neck, he dug in his spurs and took off at a gallop back toward town. As the rifle banged again, the others looked at one another, and rode out after him.

Blackie's eyes flashed. "Alright, bitch," he said, his voice hoarse with anger. "You haven't seen the last of me."

He swung into the saddle. The rifle fired again; he ducked and put spurs to his horse. They disappeared. With a clatter of hoofbeats a dark shape went by: another horse and rider, following them.

She picked herself up, shaken and upset. Her face burned where he'd slapped her, though apart from that she was unhurt. But the incident had badly frightened her, and now here she was, on foot and alone.

Unwilling to follow the gunmen, although that was the way back to town, she turned to walk back to her father's house. She'd be safest there, and in the morning... In fact, she didn't know what she'd do in the morning.

Go back to Memphis, maybe. She'd be safe there. This place was savage, full of men who behaved like wild beasts and worse. It was no place for her.

Trudging along, thinking these thoughts, she became aware of a sound ahead, coming toward her. Panicked, she left the road, and crouched among some brush, as a horse and carriage came into sight. The horse was a great black mare, magnificent, and the open carriage was luxury itself, gleaming black, with brass fittings and leather-covered seats. The driver pulled up next to her, and shone a lantern her way.

"Madam, I bid you good evening," he said in a rich, cultured voice whose inflections were obviously foreign. "I beg you, do not be afraid. May I be of service?"

She stepped out into the light, trying to compose herself. "Excuse me," she said. "I –I was frightened. A gang of men..."

"Yes, I regret I did not arrive quite in time to spare you their attentions," he said, climbing down from the carriage. "You are unhurt, I trust?"

He was a tall man with a strikingly handsome face. Somewhere between forty-five and fifty years old, perhaps, he wore a moustache and a close-cropped beard, and his hair was cut short. His eyes were penetrating and his forehead high and broad, the whole suggesting culture and intelligence. He wore a top hat and an expensive-looking suit, but he had a revolver in his waistband and a rifle in its scabbard on the carriage. Holding up the lantern, he scrutinized her closely.

"I see that one of them struck you," he said quietly. "A flogging would be salubrious for such a man." He gestured toward the carriage. "May I offer you a ride? Anywhere you may wish. I am at your disposal."

"Yes," she said, feeling instinctively that she could trust him. "Thank you. I was driving into town, but those... those men accosted me, and ran off my horse and wagon."

He offered his hand, and helped her climb up. "As for that," he said, "do not worry, my man will retrieve it for you. In fact, unless I am mistaken, here he is now."

She heard it then, too; in a moment, a man dressed all in black rode into sight, leading her horse and the buckboard. He drew up and touched his hat politely, but she could not see his face.

"Very good," the man beside her said. "And now, where is it you would like to go –into town?"

"I guess so," she answered slowly. "I was going to take a room at the hotel and get something to eat, but those men headed that way...

"I assure you, madam, that they will not bother you again. To town, then?"

She nodded, and they set off, riding for a time in silence. Her heart gradually slowed and she regained her composure. When he saw that she had calmed somewhat from the misadventure, he said, "Madam, permit me to introduce myself: my name is Ernst von Steiner."

"I am very pleased to meet you, Mister von Steiner," she said, feeling that this didn't sound quite right. "I am much obliged to you."

"Nonsense!" von Steiner said. "Why, it is a pleasure for me to do a lady even such a small service. Indeed, I am indebted to those rascals for providing me with the opportunity. It is a debt I shall be most happy to honor," he added, smiling to himself. "But enough. How came you to the Territory, miss..."

"Hayworth," she said. "Susan Hayworth. I just arrived from Memphis this morning. I came here to settle the estate of my father."

"Your father," von Steiner repeated. "Are you the daughter of that Hayworth who made such a strike in silver?"

"Yes," she said. "Did you know my father?"

His face darkened. "No, I had not that honor. My work keeps me occupied most of the time. But it is a very small community, and one hears things. Please accept my condolences, Miss Hayworth."

"Thank you," she said simply. The town was close now: she could hear the music of the dancehalls, the shouts and rough laughter of men, and every so often a gunshot. She shook her head: the place was so wide-open and lawless, she didn't know what she'd do if she met the gang of men again. The thought was worrying.

They pulled up in front of the hotel and he helped her get down. The man leading her horse and wagon pulled up beside them.

"Take the horse to the livery stable and see that it's cared for," von Steiner said to him. "After that, see that there are no further... incidents. Miss Hayworth will be stopping in town."

"Very good, Baron," he said, and rode on.

Reassured, she turned to him. "Baron?" she asked.

He nodded slightly. "In the old country I was a baron. Such titles mean little here." He bowed. "Madam, I will bid you goodnight. But I wonder... if I might pass by your father's home some time, just to see how you are getting on."

She smiled. "That would please me very much, Baron."

He bowed again. "So: *auf wiedersehen*, madam." He remounted the carriage and she watched him drive away.

A baron! Who would believe such a thing?

*   *   *

She took a room, and found a restaurant still open for supper. All the time she was on the street she was on her guard, watching over her shoulder. But she saw nothing of Blackie or the rest, and passed a quiet night.

In the morning she retrieved the horse and wagon and drove south again. Out on the road she was nervous and apprehensive, aware of her isolation, but nothing happened; again, the men who'd accosted her the night before were nowhere to be seen.

She had provisions this time, and intended to stay at the place; she'd even bought a derringer, making sure the man showed her how to load and clean it. In a way, it was foolish: she'd scarcely ever even fired a gun; but that was back home, where there was law and order. Things were different here. And every time she thought of Blackie, anger and shame flushed through her, as if she'd been sullied by his touch. She had no intention of letting that happen again, come what may.

The house seemed less lonely and forlorn, or maybe she was just getting used to it. She walked through again, taking a mental inventory, and noting particularly a double-barreled shotgun, with a box of shells. Like the derringer, having it handy just gave a body some peace of mind. Her father's bedroom was sparsely furnished and held nothing of interest. She went back downstairs and spent some time looking through his books. He'd been a practical man: she found no novels of Walter Scott, no works of history or volumes of poetry. Most of the books were of a technical nature: geological treatises, detailed atlases and maps, works on mining techniques, hydraulics, steam-driven machinery and the like. She wondered if he'd ever read a book for pleasure in his life. Although she'd thought to keep his library as a sort of memento, now she wondered if it was worth the trouble. He must have spent his entire intellectual energy on the mines.

Mightn't she have expected as much? All his life, he'd seemed to have something to prove. He'd told her once that her mother's family had never approved of him. They were a genteel lot from Boston, wealthy and snobbish, and they'd looked down on him and his modest origins. Of her mother, he rarely spoke, holding her memory in such reverence that he would not profane it even with their child. But he'd pursued his ends so tenaciously, with such single-mindedness, that she suspected, even years after her mother's death, he was still trying to show himself worthy of her.

She went back outside and stood again for a time by the grave. Maybe they were together now. She would have liked to think so. But the injustice of it all struck her once again. His life's work had come to nothing, because of another man's greed. As she looked at the still-raw earth of his grave, dry now but bare even of grass, she knew she had to do something.

She went back inside. She'd found nothing upstairs, nor in the kitchen or dining room, and she'd looked through the books. There remained the desk.

The key was still in the lock, and she opened it. A certain disorder showed it had already been searched. She wondered what had been found. Going through the contents quickly, she saw little of consequence: a few uninteresting letters; a sheaf of notes in a large envelope, some yellow with age; an empty ledger-book, its spine still new and unbent; pens and pencils, a scissors, blank paper, a ruler and compass... She smiled to herself, reached into a certain cubbyhole and pushed a secret catch. A hidden drawer opened easily.

As a curious little girl, she'd found this secret drawer. Her father had caught her going through it. He'd been severe, but she suspected that, privately, he'd been amused by her acumen. Now she removed its contents, almost sure that she was the only one who knew of their existence: several ledgers, neatly filled with entries and columns of figures, and what appeared to be a working diary or record of the mine.

A couple of hours later she felt certain that not only had her father become rich here, but that he had died in possession of his fortune. The story of his gambling losses could only be a cover for the banker who wanted to defraud the estate of what represented a huge sum. But how to proceed? Doubtless the records she'd found were dangerous – and not only to the bank. She thought of the lawyer's warning, and wondered now: those men who had accosted her the night before, were they simply ruffians harassing an unescorted woman? Or were they thugs hired by the bank to scare her off? Hadn't that Blackie said something about folks not liking a woman messing in their business?

She returned all the documents to the secret drawer and closed it again. Clearly she would have to think carefully about what to do next.

Noises came from the lane: hoofbeats, and the sound of wheels. She closed the desk and relocked it, then picked up the shotgun and checked the load. Now footsteps were coming. She slipped to a window and peeked out.

The magnificent horse and carriage told her it was the Baron. Relieved, and rather pleased, she set the shotgun in the corner and went out on the porch.

He was dressed elegantly in a morning coat with a dove-grey vest and a white silk cravat, and he swept off his top hat and bowed when he saw her.

"Miss Hayworth, what a pleasure," he said warmly. "I hope you will forgive this interruption. I was passing by on my way home, and thought I might stop to inquire of your health."

She smiled. "Baron, the pleasure is all mine."

"You are too kind. Did you pass a restful night at the hotel?"

"Yes, I did."

"And you've had no further... trouble?"

"No, none at all. Baron, won't you come in?"

He bowed again. "Forgive me, madam, but I have pressing work, nor do I wish to interrupt yours. But I wonder if you would do me the honor of dining with me this evening? My chef was trained in Paris; I can promise you a good table."

"I'd be delighted."

"Splendid! I'll have my man pick you up." He looked at his watch. "Say, seven o'clock?"

"Fine."

He saluted her again and remounted the carriage. She waved as he drove off, then went back inside.

Dinner at his home! Why, it sounded perfectly marvelous, and for a moment the anticipation of it drove her cares from her mind. She went to see about something to wear, feeling rather like a young girl invited to a cotillion. But she didn't mind the feeling at all.

*   *   *

Just before seven the carriage returned, driven this time by a coachman in a long coat and stovepipe hat. Bowing profoundly as she approached, he helped her up, remounted, and snapped the reins, all without saying a word. This rather severe silence struck her as its own sort of luxury, and she sat back and settled herself, determined to enjoy it all to the fullest.

The sun was already over behind the mountains and the air was cooling rapidly. They followed the road south away from town, so everything was new to her, and she regarded the landscape with interest. This wild and gorgeous scene was so unlike anything back in Tennessee, she might have been in another world. But they'd not gone more than a few miles when they turned off again.

She'd wondered what the home of a baron would be like, but nothing could have prepared her for the reality. The lane brought them to a stone wall topped with spikes; they passed through a gate and came into the grounds. And she gasped in wonder.

Though not terribly large, you might first have called it a castle. Like the sort of French château she had seen in illustrated magazines, it had towers with conical roofs, great windows and doors, and playful crenellations atop the walls. The carriage pulled up in front of the entrance and the coachman alighted, to help her down. A lovely young Mexican girl in a white dress opened the door and showed her in. Two suits of armor were poised like sentries on either side of the entrance hall, and before her a great staircase led to the upper floor. Down this now came the Baron, dashing and elegant in an evening coat and tie. Taking her hand, he bowed and raised it to his lips.

They passed through an astonishing room or two and came to a comfortable sitting room decorated in what she would have described as a 'French' style. The furniture looked fit for royalty, the carpets were sumptuous and the walls covered with silk. A serving man brought a silver bucket that held a bottle of wine cooled, astonishingly, in ice. The Baron, who had been making compliments and pleasantries since her arrival –most of which she little noticed, in her amazement – interrupted himself long enough to open it. The cork came out with a pop and he poured the fizzy liquid into two delicate crystal glasses. She'd never tasted champagne before: it had a pleasingly acrid taste and made her slightly giddy.

The Baron was a charming conversationalist, and they chatted pleasantly for some time before going to dinner. The dining room was smaller than she might have supposed –she had by now sufficiently recovered her presence of mind –and she wondered at that: did he perhaps often or habitually dine alone? The meal might have suited a caliph; most of the dishes were entirely unknown to her, but not a one failed to be exquisite; and course succeeded course with the most perfect naturalness and simplicity. At the end, as they sipped syrup-thick coffee from tiny porcelain cups, she could no longer contain her admiration. "Baron!" she exclaimed. "That was simply the most delicious meal I have ever eaten."

"It is enough for me that it pleased you," he said.

The hour was already late. She felt as if she had somehow slipped into an adventure from the *Arabian Nights*. That such a person, with such a home, should be found in the West: she had no words to describe it all; the thing seemed beyond belief.

The Baron had been for some moments silent, preoccupied by thought, but now he put down his cup and said, "So, madam, by way of amusement, would you care to see a few of my toys?"

"Toys?" she repeated.

"Oh, trifles, really," he said. "As the French say, *bagatelles*. But they interest me, and you might find them amusing."

He rose, and led her to a part of the house she had not yet seen. They passed through a set of double doors into a large hall and paused. The great room was dark, but by some unseen system light appeared, dimly at first but brightening by imperceptible degrees, so that one had the impression that dawn was breaking, and night turning to day. She saw dimly the outlines of two ornamental trees, planted in large pots. In one of these something stirred, and then a bird began to sing, softly and beautifully. In a moment another joined in, and another, until soon the air was filled with the song of birds.

"Why, it's lovely," Sarah said.

But the Baron did not reply. Now, as if early morning had come, she could see clearly. Nearby, a tiny bird turned, flapped its wings, and sang melodiously. But there was something about it... She stepped closer, carefully, so as not to frighten it, but it simply went on singing. Marveling that it was so tame, she moved even closer –and now she saw that the tiny creature was made of *metal!*

She looked back to the Baron but he merely smiled. Overwhelmingly curious, she examined the tiny bird. Perfectly formed, and exhibiting the most lifelike movements, all the while singing in a beautiful, entrancing voice, the creature was clearly fashioned from what looked like sterling silver. Astonished, she turned to the Baron. "But... what is it?"

"An automaton," the Baron said. Pleasure and pride were plain to see on his face. "They are all automata, that is, mechanical devices that give the appearance of life."

"But how does it work?" she asked.

"They are very complex. Each one is different, depending upon its task. It has taken a lifetime of study and experiment to produce what you see here."

"Oh, but they're marvelous," she said. "I never even imagined such a thing."

"Come this way," he said, taking her hand. They passed beyond the trees and came to where an almost life-size figure was seated cross-legged on a low dais. Naked to the waist, and dressed East Indian fashion, in turban and loin-clout, it held in one hand a sort of flute. Before it on the dais was a small woven basket.

"The making of automata is a very ancient art," the Baron said. "It was practiced in antiquity by the Greek mathematician Hero of Alexandria, and we know from Pindar that the island of Rhodes was famous for its automata, which enlivened the streets. All those devices are of course lost. King Solomon, too, according to Jewish legend, designed a throne with mechanical animals that hailed him as he ascended it: an eagle put a crown upon his head, and a dove brought him a scroll of the Torah.

"But it is in medieval Islam that the history of modern automata begins. In the ninth century, the Banu-Musa brothers, scholars working at the House of Wisdom in Baghdad, invented an automatic flute player which is described in their *Book of Ingenious Devices*. I created this figure to honor them and their pioneering work."

He clapped his hands, and the flute player opened its eyes. The contrivance looked left, then right, and settled its gaze upon them. With its free hand it reached out and removed the lid of the basket, putting it aside. Bringing the flute to its lips, it began to play. A strange music issued from the instrument, composed of unusual harmonies and subtly pleasing dissonances, the whole effect being curiously hypnotic. Then Sarah gasped, for the wide flat head of a cobra was emerging from the basket. The awful creature rose higher and higher, all the while swaying in time to the music of the flute, and as it turned, Sarah saw its baleful eyes fixed upon hers. The music came to an end; the snake fell back into the basket; the mechanical musician replaced the lid, laid aside its instrument and closed its eyes once more.

Sarah clapped her hands, laughing in delight. The Baron smiled; and now a peacock wandered past. It paused, and fanned its tail. Astonished anew, she turned again to him; he merely nodded.

They went on, to stop before a small figure in the shape of a monk. Tonsured, he wore sackcloth with a rope belt, and sandals, and in his left hand he held a wooden cross and rosary. The Baron touched his back and he began to walk, turning every few steps at right angles, so that he went about a square, as if passing through a cloister. As he went, he struck his chest with his right arm, all the while nodding, and turning his head. From time to time, he brought the cross to his lips and kissed it.

"This figure," the Baron said, "is in homage to Juanelo Torriano, Court Clock Master to Charles V, Holy Roman Emperor. Torriano's 'Clockwork Prayer' was built about 1500 in Toledo, as a commission for Phillip II of Spain."

He sighed, his gaze distant. Sarah looked at him and he said, apologetically, "Forgive me. I constructed it to amuse a lady friend; however, I underestimated the depth and gravity of her religious feeling. For all that, I meant no offense, for the idea of God as the 'Divine Clockmaker' can, with the beginnings of Deism, be traced back to the seventeenth century, and rejects any notion of atheism."

Sarah nodded, not entirely following this argument. He showed her other marvels, including a group of monkeys, who danced in a very droll fashion, and a seated lady, dressed something like Marie Antoinette, who held an ink pen in one hand, and a writing box on her lap.

"This is La Clairvoyante," explained the Baron. "She foresees the future, and will answer questions, although at times her responses are rather ambiguous, or enigmatic. Do you want to try it? Go ahead, ask her a question."

"Well, alright," Sarah said. She composed her thoughts for a moment and, leaning forward, said lowly, "Will my father's affairs be settled in good order?"

With a sound as when a clock is about to strike, La Clairvoyante's eyes, closed until then, slowly opened, and looked into Sarah's. The effect was startling. The automaton lowered its eyes to the box, tilted its head to one side, and began to write in a graceful hand. In but a moment it finished, and handed the sheet to Sarah, who looked down and read, "*It is too soon to know.*" She laughed, not displeased.

"I see what you mean," she said to the Baron. "I suppose even a machine can't always see perfectly into the future."

"Perhaps no more than any of us," the Baron said with a smile. "In the end, I can only give them life."

He drove her back home himself, explaining that his coachman had already retired. When they arrived at her father's house, he took her hand, brought it to his lips, and asked if he might call again. Alone once more, she felt like Cinderella after the ball.

*   *   *

The next day, determined to take the bull by the horns, she drove into town early and went directly to the bank. This time it wasn't long before Northrop took her into his office.

"Well, Miss Hayworth, how are you making out?" he said pleasantly. "I trust you found all of your father's personal possessions in good order?"

"I did," she answered.

"And have you come to any decision concerning his... remains? Will you take them back with you to Memphis?"

"That I don't know. It's too soon to say."

"I see." He put his fingers together, looking at her. "Quite so. In any event, how may I be of service to you this morning?"

She looked at him carefully, remembering the cautionary advice of Martinson, the lawyer. "Mr. Northrop, this is difficult to express in a delicate way. I shall endeavor not to give offense."

One of the banker's eyes twitched. She took a breath. "It stands like this. I am in possession of certain papers that indicate that at my father's death, he was still in possession of his fortune."

"Is that so?" Northrop said coolly. He did not look pleased.

"Yes," she said, with all the firmness she could muster. "Moreover, I knew my father quite well enough to know that he would not have gambled away so much money. The very idea is absurd. I believe there are... irregularities in the signatures of the documents allegedly signing over his property to the bank."

"Irregularities?" the banker repeated loudly and in an offended tone. "Ridiculous! Miss Hayworth, do you have any idea what you are asserting? Why, you offend my honor."

"I know perfectly well what I am saying," she answered. "Mr. Northrop, those documents are fraudulent. My father's signature on them has been forged."

He was on his feet, but making a visible effort to control himself. His face was bright red and he had trouble getting his breath, the words coming out in bursts:

"This is an outrage, Miss Hayworth... And after I extended you every courtesy... Why, you impute my good reputation... Never have I heard such... I am sure you will have occasion to regret this..."

At that, she too stood up. "Mr. Northrop, are you threatening me?"

He waved a hand, all at once calm. "Miss Hayworth, I threaten no one, nor is it part of my business practice to do so. I see, however, from this unreasonable and outrageous claim on your part, that we have between us a dispute that can in no way be resolved in an amicable fashion. It remains to settle the matter in court. The bank shall expect to hear from your attorney. In the meantime, I suggest that our meeting is over!"

Driving away, toward Martinson's office, she asked herself if she had handled the situation well. She had essentially no experience in such things, and though matters now were quite out in the open, she feared she had acted too precipitately –had shown her hand too soon. Northrop was hard to figure, but in offending him, she had perhaps made a powerful enemy. But what else could she have done?

Martinson wasn't pleased. "Young lady, have you lost your mind?"

"The man's a thief. I told him so, though not in so many words. Yes, he was angry; so what? I'm angry, too."

"You have compromised yourself, Miss Hayworth, and what is worse, you have put yourself in considerable danger."

"Compromised myself? I don't see how. As for danger, Northrop is a businessman. He told me he'd see me in court."

"He'll see to it that you're dead long before then." Agitated, the old lawyer got up and looked out the window. A sudden, wracking cough bent him almost double. She looked on pityingly.

Paying no attention, he turned back, fumbling with his snuff box, and asked, "What proof do you have?"

"I have his personal ledgers, which indicate steady gains up until the day he died. I have a file of correspondence with the bank, in which there is not a single mention of any loans. I have a bankbook last updated a week before his death, showing a large balance on deposit and not a single instance of a withdrawal that would suggest heavy losses. There is perhaps the testimony of people in this town who never knew my father to gamble." At this the lawyer snorted. She went on: "As to fraud, I have sufficient examples of his signature to establish some sort of legal comparison. That is not his signature on the documents Northrop showed me!"

Martinson sighed. "Miss Hayworth, none of this represents the sort of proof that can stand up in a court of law."

"Not even the bankbook?"

"No."

"And the signatures?"

"They prove nothing."

"But you haven't even seen it –any of it!"

"That is true, but I don't believe I have to. You have nothing, Miss Hayworth. You doubt Northrop's veracity: that is all. But Northrop has records and documents –executed documents –and employees who prepared the work. What is more, he has a reputation that will serve to protect him. People know him, Miss Hayworth. No one knows you. They will tend to believe the man they know."

"But the law..."

"You put too much faith in the law," he said, and broke up in a fit of coughing, pain contorting his face. When it subsided, he said in a choked voice: "None of that is the worst of it. But you have played your hand. Despite the almost derisive nature of your 'proof', you have gone to him and declared yourself an enemy. He does not know that what you have is negligible, and will probably believe the contrary, that what you have is decisive –and damning. You have placed yourself in a position of terrible risk."

She sat quiet for a moment, thinking it over. His last statement had chilled her. "Mr. Martinson, I came to you for help."

"And here's what help I can offer: get out of town, Miss Hayworth. Leave here while you still can –before something happens to you."

She stood up. "I take it you won't handle my case."

"No," Martinson said. "You don't have a case. But even if you did, and a San Francisco attorney to handle it, you'd have hell to pay before you won. He's too big."

So that was how it stood. She went back to the wagon and headed out of town, trying to think through it all. The situation looked hopeless. Oh, the lawyer was a coward; that was obvious. But that fact didn't prevent him from being right. Was she in danger? It didn't make any sense; that wasn't the sort of thing she was used to. But Memphis and its civilized ways now seemed awfully far away.

Preoccupied, she drove along, thinking of the problem. Not far from the house, a bird flew up, and she followed its flight with her eyes, distractedly. That was when she saw the plume of smoke. She knew immediately, somehow; the presentiment was sickening. She whipped up the horse, hoping she was wrong. But now she could hear the fire, and smell it. She left the wagon at the bottom of the lane, and went up on foot.

The blaze was as hot as a furnace. She'd hoped to get the documents but it would have been suicidal to go inside. The house seemed to be burning everywhere at once; flame licked out every door and window, and the smoke touched the sky. She watched it burn, sick at heart, and recoiled when, with a crash, the roof caved in. A shower of sparks flew up and fell back to the ground.

They had done this... They'd burned her out, because they were afraid of what she had. Helpless, she raged inside. The documents, the crucial documents were gone. It was all hopeless now. Despite all the lawyer had said, she'd still believed the documents would help her. Now she had nothing.

The heat from the fire became so intense she had to back further away. Tears came to her eyes, as she watched her father's home blacken and die. Like him, soon nothing would be left.

Hoofs beat the ground behind her. She turned dully, asking herself, What now? –and saw Blackie, with two of his men. She was amazed at his nerve: how dared he come back here?

He touched the brim of his hat, smirking. "Afternoon, ma'am," he said. He gestured toward the fire. "Bad fix. Are you alright?"

"I'm fine. What do you want now?"

"Want? We don't want anything. We came to offer our assistance."

She laughed then, a short harsh laugh without humor. "Well, thank you very kindly, but I don't need any 'assistance' from you all." She looked toward the house. "I'm sure you've done more than enough already."

Her tone was cool but inside she felt panicky. She well remembered her last encounter with them. She had the derringer, but it only held two shots...

Blackie was grinning. "I'm sure I don't know what you mean, ma'am. But we don't take no offense."

"Why don't you get out of here?"

He swung down from his horse. "Shucks, if that's the way you feel about it, I'm sure we won't stay long." Now he approached her, swaggering, sure of himself and his strength. "There's just one thing, before we go."

"And what might that be?

"Your bag, Miss Hayworth." He held out a hand. "I need to have a look in your bag."

She stepped back, eyes narrowing. "You'll do nothing of the sort."

"Let's not have any trouble, Miss Hayworth. Nothing will happen to you. But I need to see that bag."

"So you're a thief, as well as an arsonist?" She spat out the words, her voice nothing but scorn –as she slipped one hand inside and grasped the derringer. But he grunted, stepping forward, and his hand knocked the bag away. The little gun went flying.

"You take some awful chances, lady," he said grimly. "You want to play with guns, you better know what you're doing. But all's I'm here for is this."

He squatted down by the bag and dumped its contents out on the ground. She stood there, furious, while he went through her things. He took the letters and papers and put them under his hat, threw the rest back in the bag, and tossed it to the ground at her feet.

"There —see? Ol' Blackie don't mean you no harm. 'Course, next time..." He leered at her. "We can take up again where we left off the other night."

"You're an animal."

He swung into the saddle, grinning, and touched his hat. "Good day to you, too, ma'am." Snickering, the three turned their horses and headed back down the lane.

She heard a shout, and the gallop of a horse. A lone gunman rode into sight. He was dressed all in black, with a black hat and a kerchief masking the lower part of his face. One of Blackie's men gave an answering shout and drew his gun. But the gunman's pistol was already in his hand and he fired twice, the shots so close together they made almost one sound. Blackie's man fell from the saddle and didn't move. Cursing, the other man drew his gun and fired at close range, even as, with a shout, Blackie spurred his horse and rode on at a gallop, disappearing down the lane.

With a dull bang, like something striking cast iron, a shot hit the lone gunman in the chest. She gasped, but he only aimed and fired. The other man fell to the ground. The man in black wheeled his horse around, looking down at the men he'd shot, then dug in his spurs. The horse shot away, down the lane and out of sight.

Sarah felt sick. She'd never seen a man killed before. Unsteady on her feet, she walked to Blackie's men, who lay where they'd fallen. Each had been shot in the heart, a welter of blood staining their shirts. Shaken, she turned away.

How had it all come to this? Nothing in her experience had prepared her for the situation in which she found herself. Theft, arson, murder... She felt something like vertigo. That brute had even threatened her: *next time*, he'd said. The thought made her shudder.

She hunted around for the derringer, thinking of Blackie's hateful face, then stood, turning it over in her hand. She hadn't really looked at it until now. It was a small thing – almost derisive, like a toy –and yet it could kill a man with one squeeze of its trigger. She raised it at arm's length and sighted. It wasn't just a lady's gun, the man at the mercantile had said: men carried them too, because they were small, and easy to conceal. The weight of it in her hand was reassuring, a little. She told herself she'd know how to use it before she had occasion to again.

But after all it didn't amount to much, did it? The house was falling in now, the fire burning itself out. Everything she'd come here for was ending in ruin. She thought of what the lawyer had said to her earlier –his fear, and unwillingness to go against Northrop. Wasn't he right after all? She should go back to Memphis, give up on it all and go home. Leave them all to their thieving and their violence. This was their world, not hers.

With a sigh she picked up her bag and started back down the lane. Evening was coming on, and now she had nowhere to stay, the few things she'd brought with her gone. She'd have to go back to town, that horrid town. But she stopped when she saw the two dead men again. They'd slipped her mind for a moment. It was shocking: that's how much life and death meant here. But she wondered: who was the man in black who had killed them?

The whole scene came back to her with terrible clarity: the first outlaw, shot from his horse while he tried to draw; and the second, who'd pulled his gun and fired. She *saw* the shot strike the man in black full in the chest. How had he survived? Anyone else would have been dead... And that *sound*... Was he wearing armor? But the thought seemed absurd.

She shook her head. It was a mystery –but his arrival had been very fortunate for her. She wondered if Blackie had gotten away. Maybe, and maybe not; but she had yet to become so hardened as to wish a man dead. Almost, but not quite.

Her horse and wagon were still at the bottom of the lane. She got up on the seat, but saw a cloud of dust coming along the road. In a moment, she recognized the Baron's carriage. He was driving fast.

"Miss Hayworth! You are unhurt? I saw the smoke, and knew it could only come from here. What has happened?"

She explained it all briefly, ending, "I'm going back to town. At the very least I have to report all this to the marshal. After that... I don't know. It all seems lost. I may be going back to Memphis."

He frowned. "Perhaps that would be best, Miss Hayworth. Only you can decide. But for the moment, I wish you would come and stay with me. You can't possibly leave today, and I don't think it would be advisable for you to stay in town, alone and unprotected."

She thought that over: he certainly had a point. She said doubtfully, "Baron, I can't... I shouldn't impose upon you."

"I beg your pardon, Miss Hayworth, but it's no imposition. I have plenty of room and there's everything you'll need. And you'll be safe there."

"But what about the marshal? Those –those men – their bodies are still up there."

"I'll send word to the marshal. Those men will wait for him."

Clearly, he was right. The town was hateful to her, anyway. He tied her wagon behind, helped her into the carriage, and they set off.

*   *   *

So she came to live at the Baron's. She intended at first only to stay the night, settle up her business and take the next train east. But she was exhausted, and when she awoke the next day in the great feather bed of her room, the morning was much advanced. Somewhat embarrassed, she found the house empty save for the Mexican girl, who told her the Baron was engaged in his workshop and had asked not to be disturbed except in event of emergency. So instead she took breakfast and wandered the grounds, and then read for a time in the library where great windows let in the air and you could hear birds singing. The Baron had volumes of Browning and Keats she'd never seen, and when she tired of reading she played on the grand piano, a superb instrument brought from Germany. In the evening she dined with the Baron as sumptuously as before. He was in fine spirits, witty and charming, perfectly attentive and gracious; and –what he had not done before –after encouraging her to talk of her earlier life and her father, he spoke of his boyhood in Switzerland. Later, lying in her deliciously soft bed, she realized she was rather infatuated with him.

A second day passed in the same way, and then another, but it disturbed her that she'd never heard from the marshal. She did not doubt that the Baron had sent word; but with two men dead and the house burned down, didn't the marshal want a statement from her? The morning of the fourth day she rose early, but the Baron had already shut himself away with his work. She wanted to tell him her plans, but hated to disturb him; so after breakfast she had the horse hitched to the buckboard and drove into town.

The marshal looked very little pleased to see her. Yes, the Baron had sent a note. The marshal had seen to it that the bodies were removed, and buried at Boot Hill. He must have seen the surprise in her face, for he added, more callously than necessary, "All that kind end up there." She just looked at him.

"I done that because it needed doing," he went on. "But you've got to realize that what happened at that house is out of my jurisdiction."

"I beg your pardon, marshal?"

"Out of my territory." He waved a hand toward the street. "I'm the marshal of the *town*, Miss Hayworth. Your father's property isn't in town. I've got no authority to do anything there."

"I see," she said. "Tell me, who does have authority?"

He made a wry face. "A federal marshal, I guess. Good luck finding one who can help you. The fact is, the house is burned down and two outlaws are dead, and there just ain't anybody much to do anything about it."

"What about their leader –Blackie?"

"Got nothing on him. You say he come riding up while the house was on fire. Ain't nothing says he set it."

"He stole my letters –and threatened me."

"Did he hurt you?"

"No, but..."

"Listen," the marshal said, interrupting her and holding up one hand. "Blackie Lancaster is a hard man, a bad man to tangle with. He don't come to town too often, and that's how we like it, 'cause he's mean as a rattlesnake and fast with his gun. You'd do best to shy clear of him. But I've got nothing on him except you felt threatened by him and you say he took some letters, and that ain't enough. And on top of it all, none of this happened in town. So stay out of his way."

Back out on the street, half-blinded by the glare of the sun, she didn't know why she'd bothered to go to the marshal at all, just to hear that. It had begun to seem that dishonest men did whatever they pleased in this town, and everyone else just had to make out as best they could.

She wanted a few things from the mercantile, but avoided the bank, not wanting a confrontation; nor did she care to see the lawyer again. Once she had what she needed, she drove out again, beginning to despise the dusty little town and the people who lived there, and wondering why she stayed on. Weren't things finished here, or as good as, and wouldn't she be better off back in Memphis? Yet for some reason she had not left. Certainly, it seemed wrong to give up on it all, and allow the fortune her father had amassed to be stolen by unscrupulous men. Yet without proof the wrong could not be redressed, and she had to acknowledge that, now, what proofs she had were gone. It all seemed hopeless.

The day was fine and clear, but, preoccupied with her thoughts, she was all but oblivious to it. Instead, as she drove, her mind seemed to go in circles, round and round, without finding any answer. And the blackened shell that now stood beside her father's still-fresh grave seemed a mute accusation of them all –including her.

Passing it, she had a troubling sensation, as if she were being watched.

The road stretched on, dusty and empty. She picked up the pace, wanting to get back, but ahead of her, a man on horseback appeared, walking his horse from a copse of trees. Her heart sank: it was Blackie.

She looked around but saw no one. He rode slowly toward her as she drew up and waited. He had the same arrogant grin on his face and he rode easy in the saddle, confident and relaxed.

"Howdy, Miss Hayworth," he said, touching the brim of his hat, just as he had the last time, four days before. To her, this mockery of politeness was nothing but contempt in disguise. "Hello, Blackie," she answered, trying to keep her tone even.

"Nice day for a drive," Blackie said, glancing around. Did she detect a certain wariness in that glance?

"Yes, I suppose it is."

"It's a shame," he went on, "that such a pretty woman has to drive into town all alone."

"I don't mind. It gives me a chance to think."

"No, really, it's a shame. A person has to be careful." He went on, as if enjoying the sound of his own talk: "A woman, for instance. She doesn't know what might happen. She doesn't know who she might run into. It could be *dangerous*."

For a moment, she just looked at him. The insolence in his face was so intolerable, she would have liked to slap him. But obviously he wanted to provoke some reaction. At length, she said, "It is indeed a dangerous country. I have seen that all too well. And violence only fosters violence. You, too, Blackie, you're alone today. It was a pity what happened to your friends."

A dark look crossed his face; she saw this was the wrong thing to have said. He moved closer, his eyes hard. "A pity," he repeated. "Get this, Miss Hayworth: your fancy talk and Eastern ways don't cut no ice with *me*. I told you last time I seen you that the next time..." He grabbed a handful of her hair, pulling her to him, and forced his mouth onto hers.

When he finally let her go, she slapped him, hard. His eyes flashed and he grinned, with no humor, and slapped her back. She saw stars, and put a hand to her face, stung by the roughness of his hand. He kissed her again, even more brutally.

"You listen, bitch," he said when at last he let her go. "You think you're too good for ol' Blackie, but I'm going to take you off your high horse."

"I don't think so," a man's voice said. With a curse, Blackie turned, and Sarah gasped.

Standing next to Blackie's horse was the gunfighter – the man in black. Where he'd come from, Sarah couldn't imagine. Blackie's face twisted and he went for his gun. It was clearing leather when the gunfighter's left hand shot out and closed like a vise around Blackie's wrist. Blackie's jaw clenched and his face turned almost purple, but he couldn't move his hand. The gunfighter pried the Colt from Blackie's fingers with his free hand, and threw it away.

"You need a lesson in manners," he said. "We'll start with how to treat a lady."

He took hold of Blackie, dragged him from the saddle and threw him down. Blackie hit the ground so hard he lay unmoving for a moment, stunned. The gunfighter gave a shout and slapped Blackie's mount on the rump. The horse whinnied and galloped away. The gunfighter turned back to the outlaw, waiting. Blackie was slow to get up: he got to his hands and knees, shaking his head. Impatient, the gunfighter bent over and hauled him to his feet. The outlaw snarled, but there was doubt in his eyes, as if he were beginning to be afraid. He sized up the gunfighter, stepped in and threw a right. The gunfighter blocked it easily and punched Blackie in the stomach. Blackie went over like he'd been hit with an axe handle. He straightened painfully, then rushed the gunfighter, swinging both fists. The other man brushed off the blows and swung his right to Blackie's chin. Sarah saw the bone break, the lower jaw sliding sideways; she cried out, horrified. Blackie went down like a felled ox and lay unconscious in the middle of the dusty road.

"Is he dead?" she asked, leaning over to look; but she could see his chest move as he breathed.

"No," the gunfighter said. "He'll live."

He got his arms under Blackie and dragged him to the side of the road. "He'll be a little the worse for wear," he said. "But his horse didn't go far. When he comes to, he can go home and lick his wounds." He turned to Sarah solicitously. "But what of you, ma'am? Are you alright?"

"Yes, I'm fine," she said. "He didn't hurt me, just... I was frightened, that's all." She laid a hand on the gunfighter's arm. "I want to thank you. I don't know what I would have done if... if you hadn't helped me."

He touched his hat brim. "Don't mention it, ma'am. It's what any decent man would have done."

He looked around. "Well, it's pretty hot out here, and you've had about enough excitement for one day. Let's get you back to the Baron's."

He tied his horse behind the buckboard and climbed up on the seat beside her, taking the reins. They set off.

"So you know the Baron," she said.

"Oh, yes," he answered.

For a time they drove in silence. She was struck by his calm quiet demeanor, his air of self-assurance. He might have been about her own age, but she wasn't sure. He was clean-shaven, and his chestnut-colored hair was cut short. His blue eyes were quick and intelligent, set in a handsome face, tanned by sun and wind. His clothes were simple, almost plain, though made of good material; and his hand-tooled boots looked expensive but well worn-in. She wondered about him: he seemed so different from the others she had met.

The Baron's home wasn't far. They pulled up in front, and he jumped down and lifted her out as though she weighed no more than a feather. The feel of his strong gentle hands on her waist was so nice it almost made her blush.

"Go ahead on in, ma'am," he said. "I'm sure the Baron is waiting for you."

She glanced toward the great house. "Wait," she said. "I don't even know your name."

But he'd already climbed up on the seat and was driving away.

*   *   *

In fact, the Baron was standing at a window in the entrance hall. "Ah, Sarah," he said. "I see you've been to town."

"Yes, I have," she answered. "I'm afraid I've had a bit of an adventure." She related the events of the day, ending with her rescue by the gunman in black. "Who is he, Baron? He said he knew you."

"Oh, yes," the Baron said. "He works for me." The answer had a certain finality, and Sarah said no more.

That night at dinner, he asked if she played chess. "Only very indifferently," she replied. "I know how the pieces move, and I understand the basic principles of the game, but I'm afraid I'm a rather poor strategist."

After dinner, he asked her to play the piano. But when they went into the library, she saw a strange new apparatus.

"This," he said with an air of modesty that did not conceal his pride, "is the Turk. It is a chess-playing machine."

In fact, the device consisted of a life-size figure of a man with a black beard and grey eyes, dressed in Turkish robes and a turban, which was seated behind a large cabinet with a chessboard on top. The Turk's left hand held a long tobacco pipe; the right arm was at rest next to the board.

"In its form, this automaton is, again, an homage," the Baron said. "The original *Schachtürke* was constructed in 1770 by Wolfgang von Kempelen, an author and inventor from Pressburg, in the Hapsburg Empire. Von Kempelen's intention was to entertain the court of the Empress Maria Theresa of Austria, and in this he succeeded admirably. Exhibited by its several owners until it unfortunately perished in a fire in 1854, it won the greater part of the games played during its demonstrations, and defeated such opponents as Napoleon Bonaparte and Benjamin Franklin. Unfortunately, the original Turk was a fraud."

At a look from Sarah, he nodded. "Yes, a fake, an elaborate hoax. Not a true automaton at all, but rather an ingenious bit of trickery –a mechanical illusion, if you will. The cabinet appeared to be full of gears and cogs, like clockwork. In fact, this machinery concealed a human chess master hidden inside, who operated the apparatus. My machine, on the contrary..."

"You don't mean it can actually play chess," Sarah said, incredulous.

"Oh, yes," the Baron replied. "The Turk represents a great step forward in my researches. Up to the point when I began work upon it, I had limited myself to the appearance of life. As such, it is largely a matter of motion and sound, rendered as lifelike as possible –as in my other creations that you have seen. I flatter myself that the results have shown a certain success. With the Turk, I embarked upon a far greater challenge: to create a machine capable of reasoning, analysis, drawing conclusions, and proposing itself a course of action – in short, a machine that could think."

"Why, that's incredible," Sarah said.

The Baron made a slight nod. "Its field is limited. It gives no political discourses, writes no philosophical treatises. It only plays chess. For me, the scope of the problem was manageable –as a sort of first essay, if you will. In creating a machine capable of thought, chess is an ideal beginning. The problem, you see, is well defined both in terms of the operations that are allowed –that is, the moves of the pieces – and in the ultimate goal, which is checkmate of the opponent. The game is neither too simple nor too difficult, and since, generally speaking, chess is considered to require 'thinking' for skillful play, the successful realization of a chess-playing machine forces one to admit the possibility of mechanized thinking. And indeed, once I made the first real breakthrough, solved the basic problem as it were, I was primarily hindered by my own shortcomings in the game. Oh, I have played all my life, but I am in no sense a master. Nonetheless, I did my best; and aided by the study of certain classics in the literature, the machine plays a very passable game. In fact..."

"Yes?" Sarah said.

The Baron shrugged. "It mostly plays far better than I. It has... learned."

"It's all so unbelievable," Sarah mused. "A machine that can think!" She walked closer, studying it. Intrigued, she turned back to the Baron. "Will you show me?"

He bowed slightly. "I'm happy to oblige. Do you wish to play?"

"No, no," she said. "Please –you play it. I'll watch."

Now began a fascinating demonstration. From a drawer in the cabinet, the Baron removed a red and white ivory chess set, which he arranged on the board.

"By tradition," he said, "the Turk plays white and has the first move. In practice, it makes little difference." He touched a part of the mechanism. The Turk opened its eyes and looked left and right. Sarah found its expression very droll, and tried not to giggle. With a clockwork noise, like gears turning, the Turk's right arm rose stiffly and shifted to a position over the board. Its hand opened and came down on the King's Pawn, which it grasped and moved forward two squares. The hand rose again and returned to its original place, as the gears were heard to turn once more. The Baron countered the move and turned to Sarah.

"All this noise is quite unnecessary," he said, "and is really only a bit of humor on my part. In the original device, when the Turk made a move, one heard a clockwork sound, which added to the illusion of machinery. My mechanism is in fact perfectly silent."

The Turk made its move, and the Baron frowned slightly. He countered again, and the Turk immediately moved once more.

"The machine plays an aggressive game," the Baron said, almost to himself. And indeed, the Turk took almost no time to reflect, but made its moves directly after those of the Baron, as if it had already foreseen the Baron's strategy, and was prepared to counter it.

Soon the Baron was completely absorbed, and spoke no more. Sarah was struck by the strangeness of this spectacle, wherein a man attempted to better a machine he had himself created. It shortly became evident to her that the game was not going well for the Baron. He had already lost a number of important pieces when after a move by the Turk, she heard him mutter something in what had to be German.

Two moves later, to a whirring of gears, the Turk's mouth opened and a stern, whispering voice said, "*Échec!*"

The Baron made another move. The Turk's mouth opened again; again it whispered, "*Échec!*"

The Baron sighed and tipped over his king in surrender. The Turk looked left and right again, seeming to smile in triumph before closing its eyes once more. The Baron turned away, holding up his hands as if to say, What can one do?

Sarah clapped her hands, delighted. "Oh, that was just wonderful," she said. "But tell me, what did he say?"

"Say?" the Baron repeated, distracted. "Oh, he said '*échec*' –French for 'check'."

"It's marvelous," Sarah said, still enthused. "And he won the game! I would never have thought it possible."

"Yes," the Baron said. "If only all of my efforts were crowned with such success."

She looked at him to see if he were joking, but his face was perfectly serious. Still, she could not be entirely sure.

*   *   *

The following day, the Baron was again occupied in his workshop. The morning was fine, and as she strolled in the garden after breakfast, it seemed that the heat of the summer was passing away; it would be cool weather soon. How long had she been here? By the calendar, not long, though so much had happened. She wondered anew if she should be leaving. She had little reason to go, but if anything even less to stay, aside from a certain disinclination to depart, which she found hard to account for. Her business was unresolved yet at a standstill, and so much to her disadvantage she could scarcely see how the situation might change. She seemed to have done nothing but make enemies –powerful, dangerous enemies. Yet, to her recollection, before coming here she'd never had an enemy in her life. The thought was disturbing.

But the day was too pretty to brood. To distract herself, get away a bit, she decided to take a ride. She went back in and asked Maria about it. The girl assured her it would be no trouble to have a horse saddled and brought round for her.

To her surprise, she found the gunfighter waiting with it, a beautiful bay. His own was beside it, saddled and ready. He gave her a hand, and mounted up. "Where to?" he said.

"Oh, anywhere," she answered, feeling awkward. "I just thought I would take a ride. You don't have to come with me. I don't want to take you away from your work."

"Don't you worry about that." He grinned at her. "Part of my work is making sure you don't run into any trouble."

She smiled, unsure what to say, and they rode out, going easy. He led her on a trail up the mountain, away from the town, and soon they'd reached a fair elevation. The rocky, broken land stretched away beneath them, beautiful and remote.

"Oh, it's fine," she said, looking away into the distance.

"It's pretty country," he agreed, "as long as you stay clear of where they're mining, which ruins it."

They pushed on up, Sarah enjoying the view. The gunfighter didn't speak much, but she liked being with him; even his silence was companionable. She admired his lean, hard figure, his broad strong shoulders and narrow hips, and the easy way he sat his horse. She imagined she must seem very citified to him. But as they stood looking down and away from a broad ledge, giving the horses a rest, he said, "I notice you don't ride side-saddle."

"No," she said. "My father taught me to ride, and he called such as that foolishness. He said if a person was going to ride, he or she had best ride properly, whether man or woman."

The gunfighter nodded. "I'd have to say that to my mind he was right." After a pause, he went on: "He sounds like a remarkable man. Tell me about him –I mean, if you want to."

So she did, generally at first; but then, before she knew it, she had told him all about her mother, her childhood, even her marriage, and her father's departure for the west. She found herself surprised to be so open, so frank. But he listened carefully, occasionally asking a question, but mostly in silence, as if he wanted to learn it all, from her own lips.

The telling had gone on so long that they were back almost before she had finished. In front of the Baron's home once more, she dismounted and he took the reins of her horse. She paused, looking up into his face. "I want to thank you," she said. "I've had a lovely time."

He touched the brim of his hat. "Oh, no, Miss Hayworth," he said, smiling. "The pleasure has been all mine."

He was setting off when she said, "Wait! I don't even know your name."

"That's alright," he said. "I don't have one."

She went back in the house wondering at that, for it seemed a curious pleasantry. But she found the Baron inside, looking out the window. He asked if she'd enjoyed her ride, but he seemed distracted, perhaps even discontent, so that he hardly listened to her answer. She guessed that he preferred to be alone, and excused herself. As she rested upstairs in her room, her thoughts kept returning to the gunfighter. Though they came from two different worlds, she felt easy and comfortable around him. She experienced none of the social distance and the distinction of class that, rightly or wrongly, she felt with the Baron, despite all his courtesy and congenial hospitality. And yet the Baron was a peaceful man, whose background was civilized and cultured, not unlike her own. He had none of the almost casual violence of the gunfighter – violence that shocked and frightened her, and yet, when employed in her defense, thrilled her in some secret and mysterious recess of her heart. The gunfighter was a mystery, a cipher: how could a man so gentle and kind be capable of such violence? She would have liked to know more about him, to understand him better.

That night at dinner she asked the Baron about him, mentioning his strange answer to her question.

"What?" the Baron said. "His name? Why, I'm sure... He must have been joking. Of course he has a name. His name is Young... James Young."

"I wonder why he wouldn't tell me himself."

"Oh, it's his... his sense of humor, I suppose. You know, Miss Hayworth," he went on, looking into his wineglass as he composed his thoughts. "Mr. Young is a... an unusual man. He has a great capacity for violence."

She looked at him, trying to read his meaning. "Yes, Baron, I... I know you're right. He protected me from that outlaw Blackie Lancaster. In fact, he *saved* me. If he hadn't been there, Blackie would have..." She dropped her eyes, embarrassed. "Blackie would have assaulted me. But, thank Heaven, Mr. Young was there. He beat Blackie down with his fists. I don't think Blackie will be bothering anyone else, at least for a while." She looked up at him: he seemed to be watching her very closely. "But you don't think Mr. Young would hurt *me*, do you, Baron?"

"No," he answered after a moment. "No, I don't think so."

Later, she played the piano while the Baron played chess again. But his mind must not have been on the game, for the machine defeated him after only a few moves, and he quitted the smiling Turk in disgust.

*   *   *

So began the pattern of the next few days: during the afternoon she took a ride with James Young; and in the evening she dined with the Baron, afterwards playing the piano while he read, or smoked, or played chess with the Turk. The Baron seemed to have become accustomed to her presence. He spoke to her sometimes of his work, though she was never exactly sure what he was working on, and in general he became a good deal less formal, even to the point where he no longer concealed his mood. No one could have said that with her he was anything less than a perfect gentleman; but she saw now that, at moments, something weighed upon his mind, or at least seemed to cause him some concern. But he did not take her into his confidence, nor did she presume to question him. At other moments he was carefree, almost gay, and she came to believe that success or failure in his work determined his humor.

With James things were different. From the beginning, she had felt easy and comfortable in his presence, and soon it seemed that all distance between them had been effaced. With him, she could say anything, talk of anything; and their conversations touched on the most intimate facets of her life. Of himself, he spoke little, and in general he was not a great talker. Mostly she talked, and he listened; he was a fine listener. She wondered, at times, that he cared to speak so little of himself; but she knew that men were naturally less gregarious than women, and moreover she was hardly surprised that a man who had lived by his gun should not wish to recall the past. But sometimes at night, as she drifted off to sleep, she wondered about him. Where did he come from? Who were his people? What had been his life, and how had he come to be a gunfighter? And what was his association with the Baron? Would she ever know?

But she had not given up on her own affairs, and one day she asked James to take her to see the mine.

She could tell immediately that the request did not please him. He didn't answer at first, just turned his eyes away and gazed off into the distance. She waited, expecting him now to refuse, and wondering what argument might persuade him to change his mind. Instead, speaking slowly, he said, "You take advantage of me, Sarah. Surely you know I can't refuse you anything, and yet you ask me the one thing I ought to refuse."

She waited, thinking there must be more; and indeed, after a pause, he went on: "You understand this is absolutely contrary to my instructions."

"I don't understand," she said.

"The Baron," he answered. "I have instructions from him concerning you. I am to do anything you want, take you anywhere you please —except there. The Baron was explicit about that."

She nodded, thinking it over. "That's fine, James. I understand. Believe me, I don't want you to do anything to jeopardize your place with the Baron. We'll just forget that I asked. I'll go myself."

"For heaven's sake, Sarah." It was the first time he'd ever seemed cross, or used an irritated tone with her, and she was surprised. "Don't you understand? If the Baron doesn't want me to take you there, it's because it's dangerous!"

She had to smile at that. "James, I appreciate your concern —yours, and the Baron's. But I want to see it —no, it's more than that, I have to see it. That mine was my father's life. And now they've taken it. You don't think I can just forget about it all, do you?"

He didn't answer. She felt bad. "Don't worry over it," she said. "You have to do as the Baron wants. I'll ride over myself. I just want a look-see. What is it they say? —I want to see the elephant."

He shook his head, but apparently her determination carried the question. Without another word, he brought around two horses, and they set off.

The various mines were located east of town. They headed cross-country, and soon were passing through an area where the miners and prospectors were working their claims. All around was the chink of picks and shovels, and each little encampment had one man on guard-duty, holding a rifle or shotgun, who watched them pass with careful, suspicious eyes. Some had given names to their claims, painted crudely on bits of old wood: *Hog-'em*, *Gouge-'em*, *Stink-'em*; and the miners were living in holes dug into the sides of the hills, in tents made of canvas or potato sack, or in shanties made from whatever had come to hand. The dusty, sweat-covered men were gouging at the hillside with picks, driving steel drilling rods with eight-pound double-jacks, yanking at the stubborn rock with crowbars; periodically a blast went off. Sarah watched a group pour a charge of blasting powder, insert a fuse, fill in sand and ram it down, then light the fuse and run. The concussion made her ears ring. With the explosion rock and smoke shot into the air. The rock rained down again, and the men went back to pick through the ore. Some stopped and stared at her as she rode by, but most were too preoccupied with the work to notice.

"Most of the ore near the surface is gone," James said to her. "The big mines have had to drive deep. But hope dies hard."

Sarah shook her head. These men, scrabbling so intently over the broken hillside, seemed to her like so many ants, intent on forcing a living from the harsh, infertile land.

Now they heard a confused roar, a sort of rumbling, clanking, clanging and grinding all at once. It intensified as they came over a rise and saw, sprawled below them, a number of low wooden buildings connected by hard-packed dirt roads. A group of men were standing near a tallish structure at the center, itself connected by heavy chains to a shed whose smokestack gave forth a stream of thick black smoke. Beside it was a pile of cinders yards across. A team of wagons loaded with ore was driving slowly away with a cracking of whips. Sarah counted eight or nine pairs of mules –it was hard to say, with all the dust. James pulled up and she stopped by him.

"There it is," he said. He had to raise his voice to make himself heard. "That's it, the Hard Luck Mine."

It didn't look like much, certainly not like a fortune in precious metal –rather a bunch of weather-beaten buildings that had never known paint, bleached grey by the relentless sun. She patted her face with a kerchief, for the afternoon heat had built up, and said, "Why are those men waiting there?"

"They're fixing to go to work," James answered. "The shift is about to change. The mines work around the clock. The tall structure is the hoisting works –the head of the shafts, where they bring the ore out, and move the miners up and down." And even now, as the chains clanked back and forth, men were emerging from the hoists. They looked just like those waiting except freshly dirty with sweat and dust and the drip of underground water. All wore more or less the same clothing –battered felt hat, short-sleeve undershirt, baggy trousers that seemed about to fall off, and boots –but the ones leaving had such an air of fatigue that Sarah felt a touch of pity for them. She imagined the works below, the shafts driving deep into subterranean darkness, the men laboring to the point of exhaustion, burrowing out the mountainside a shovelful at a time. Now the exodus had finished, the exhausted miners tramping away in the direction of town, and the mine began to swallow the fresh shift, two and three at a time. She pictured them below, toiling in the eternal night by oil lamps and candlelight, like moles. It gave her a shiver, of loathing and horror.

"The Hard Luck," she said, musing. "It certainly seems aptly named."

He looked at her. "It's made a few men –a very few – quite rich. Others..." He gestured vaguely toward the men slowly walking away. "Others earn a living wage, more or less. The pay is good, though the work is killingly hard. Of course, the more dangerous work pays even better."

"It is dangerous, isn't it," she said vaguely, her mind turning it all over. He gave a short laugh.

"The only safe place is above ground," he said. "Maybe not always there."

"He was down there, I guess," she said, talking to herself.

"What's that?"

She looked up, a profound sadness on her face. "My father," she said bleakly. "He must have been down there... when he was killed in the accident."

"Accident?" James asked. She looked at him, questioningly. He seemed to realize his mistake and looked away, into the distance. She waited, and said at last, "Was there something you wanted to say?"

"No," he said. "There's just... Well, there's all sorts of accidents."

At that moment, it seemed, she understood; and she saw that she should have understood long before. There'd been no accident.

She began to cry, bitter tears that she couldn't stop. She'd held them back a long time, but this was too much; it overwhelmed her and she couldn't help herself. The grief was still there, an awful aching grief like a void inside her; and too she felt indignation, and loathing for a world where such things might be –for the evil that so deeply scarred men's hearts.

He reached out and took her hand, saying nothing, as if he understood her so well, no words were necessary. They sat their horses in silence until the fit passed, and she dried her eyes, shaking her head.

"Let's go," he said gently. "If you've seen enough."

She nodded. They turned and started back. Behind them at the hoisting works, ore cars were emerging, rolling heavily along the narrow-gauge track.

Now she rode back past the miners and prospectors scrabbling at the barren hillside –rode past without looking at them, for they were become like ghosts to her, spectres whose real existence had faded quite away. Only one thing she wondered: did they have families somewhere –wives, and daughters, perhaps –who missed them? And if so, would any of them ever see one another again?

She and James rode on silently, each absorbed in thought. Soon the trail narrowed, following the broken hills, and he led the way. As they came along single-file, the trail clinging to the steep slope, with stubborn pines growing above them and a sharp drop-off below, a rattlesnake slid out in front of her horse. Frightened, the animal reared, hoofs beating the air. For a moment she held on, clinging desperately to the saddle's pommel –then lost her grip and fell, landing hard and sliding down in a shower of dust and stones. He turned at her cry, leapt off his horse, and slid down after her, to where she clung to the base of a juniper. Her ankle was turned but she smiled at him, mouth tight with pain. "Don't put any weight on it," he said, and carried her back up. His grip was gentle but she could feel the strength of his arms and hands. Back on the trail the snake was gone and the horses waited calmly. He bound up her ankle, lifted her bodily into the saddle and led her horse until the trail widened again and he could mount up.

They took it easy going back after that, and dusk was coming before they reached the Baron's.

"How is it?" he asked, helping her down.

"It hurts, but it'll be alright." She put a hand on his chest. "James, I want to thank you. If you hadn't been there..."

"You wouldn't have been there if I hadn't been with you," he said. His tone was self-accusing.

"I asked you to take me," she answered. "In fact, I insisted. And if I'd gone by myself, I might still be lying there."

"Sarah," he began, but she put her hands to his face and kissed him. His arms tightened around her and for a moment she felt peaceful and safe. When they separated he had a funny look on his face that she couldn't figure before he turned away.

"I better put up the horses," he said. "See you later."

"Okay," she said.

As she went up the steps into the house, limping, the Baron came out. His face was livid and his jaw clenched. He paused and bowed. "Miss Hayworth," he said, but hurried on. In a moment his voice rose to a shout, and she fled upstairs to her room.

*　　　　　　　*　　　　　　　*

The Baron was for the most part silent as they dined that night, and afterwards excused himself, saying he was tired from his work. She sat alone with a book in the library, her leg propped on an ottoman, reading little, mostly just musing on what she had seen and all that had taken place. In the end, she too went to bed early but sleep did not come easily.

In the morning the ankle was swollen and painful and she found herself still limping. She thought it best not to ride, and went to excuse herself to James, but he was nowhere to be found. It seemed odd.

The day dragged on, long, tiresomely hot. She'd thought fall was coming but it seemed she was wrong. Her book bored her, she had no taste for music, and she had no one to talk to, even had she felt like talking. Instead, she went aimlessly from room to room, or sat in the garden until even in the shade the heat became too oppressive. What she'd seen the day before had forced her once again to reflect, and examine her own motives. Matters were stalled, her situation was at a standstill, and she realized she'd just been letting the days pass. But she could not indefinitely continue to avail herself of the Baron's hospitality. What was more, seeing the mine had shown her what was at stake, and fanned up anew her desire for justice.

The mine... Her thoughts returned to it again and again. Like a great mechanized beast, it devoured its twice-daily portion of men, and disgorged the precious ore, all the while belching smoke and emitting its clanking, clanging din. The massive ore cars she'd seen, headed for the mills, made it all too plain why men would lie and cheat, even kill, to control the wealth they carried. She could not fight such men alone. But Martinson had made it clear he would not help her. No: she needed a skilled attorney, a man who understood mining, and was expert in commercial affairs. Perhaps in San Francisco... She would have to go there to secure representation. There would be costs: travel, retainers, fees... She hoped her limited resources would suffice.

It seemed the best plan she could devise. She composed a note to Martinson, advising him in a general way of her intentions, and asking that he prepare his files and any other documents or information that would be useful to her new counsel. The man could do that much, at least.

Almost certain that the Baron would want to help, she felt unsure how to respond. In the beginning, she'd imagined herself a little bit in love with him. Now... she didn't know. His feelings for her were equally hard to apprehend. At times, she half-believed he meant to propose to her; yet the next moment she was sure she utterly bored him. Did he love her, or was she but a traveler in need of aid, the object of a sort of charity? And even supposing he cared for her: if he proposed, would she accept? Most women wouldn't dream of refusing, but there seemed such a gulf between them, that she wondered if it might ever be bridged. And what was more, when she thought of love, her thoughts turned to James. Her feelings about him were like something hidden inside her, a flower nurtured in a secret garden of her heart. She felt instinctively that the Baron would disapprove. But her thoughts went again and again to the quiet, gentle gunfighter: how he'd leapt to help her when she fell, without a thought for himself; his arms about her, strong, protective; the kiss they'd shared... She blushed, told herself she was acting like a schoolgirl; but all that changed nothing. The violence of his life, of his very nature, she dismissed, sure now it could never be directed at her; and though the difference in their backgrounds might have been perceived by someone else as a gulf as great as that between her and the Baron, she did not see it so. She sensed something in each of them that reached out to the other, bridging any distance.

The day went by at last; night came. When she went down to dinner, she was surprised to find herself alone; but the Baron soon joined her, flushed and in seemingly high spirits –although, for some reason, it seemed to her that they might be suddenly dashed, if circumstances had it so. She wondered if he'd been drinking. Certainly he did now, glass after glass of expensive wine imported from France, which, nonetheless, seemed to affect him little.

Over dinner, she explained to him her plans, the decisions she'd taken and her proposed course of action concerning the mine. He approved of them in a general way, as one might of an idea that had little immediate application. It seemed to her that perhaps he wasn't paying a great deal of attention. Indeed, having eaten little, he began a rambling discourse.

"I have shown you a little of my work, Sarah," he said, "but of the most important part, the whole world remains ignorant. So much of it is so novel that it must almost universally be met with incomprehension –derision, perhaps – perhaps even fear. All that will change, in time. You have seen my first efforts, *mes essais* as the French say, and you applauded them; but of all in them that is tentative, provisional, or *fausse route* –of that, you have no idea. Ah, the labors they have cost me! –the false starts, the dead ends! The hours worn out, fruitlessly! All this, no one can imagine. For science, the pursuit of knowledge, is a harsh and demanding mistress. And yet her joys are... inexpressible! To find a way – discover the solution –to succeed! But then, the next day, the task begins anew..."

He rang the bell, called for champagne; when it came, he drank off a glass, and went on: "There are some who would call my work unimportant, useless inventions, tinkering. These men call themselves scientists! They are but pedants, dullards who cannot perceive even their own limitations, the worst sort of 'professor'. I have succeeded in what others could not even begin to imagine. We stand here at the dawn of a new Creation, a new Garden of Eden. For I... I have created *life... mechanical* life!"

His eyes blazed with almost infernal triumph. Had he gone mad? Certainly he was fatigued, overwrought, worn out from overwork. At a loss for what to say, Sarah stammered, "I don't understand... What do you mean?"

He drank off another glass of champagne. "It begins with Descartes," he went on, more calmly now. "In his *Description of the Human Body*, he suggests that the bodies of animals, understood to include the bodies of men, are nothing more than complex machines. Their skeletal structure, muscular system, even their organs, could all be replaced by mechanisms –cogs, wheels, pistons, cams. The mechanical is the standard to which the natural is compared. Ultimately, the universe itself may be conceived as a vast clockwork. The world is a great machine, ticking along perfectly without the intervention of any God, just as a clock continues to keep time, once set in motion, without the assistance of a clock maker. But Descartes was a coward."

He poured a third glass. "Bah! –I am too harsh. Yet he lacked the courage –I should say, the *will* –to see his conclusions to their logical end. He hesitates, compromises, arrives at last at that shabby dualism, according to which the mind and body are not identical.

"Oh! –the man was brilliant, a genius. If I am critical, it is because he saw the truth, yet finally could not accept it.

For he wrote, in his treatise on man, 'I should like you to consider that these functions (including passion, memory and imagination) follow from the mere arrangement of the machine's organs every bit as naturally as the movements of a clock or other automaton follow from the arrangement of its counter-weights and wheels.' Passion, memory, imagination! It is all there. So why this sad recourse to a dualism that explains nothing, that perceives the truth and yet, like a frightened child, hides its face and covers its eyes? No!"

He slammed a hand on the table; Sarah jumped. Much of the Baron's talk was unintelligible to her, but she was surprised by his wildness and fervor. Seeming to sense her disquiet, he gathered himself and went on in a more subdued tone:

"That, for me, was the starting-point; from there I began work. My first machines, such as the ones you have seen, gave the appearance of life. This was a beginning, but hardly satisfactory. I moved from the appearance of life to its *functions*. I built a duck that not only gives every appearance of life –it walks, flaps its wings, emits a loud quacking sound – but it does more: it eats, digests, defecates –excuse me, madam –and what it eats provides the fuel for its functions! Do you see? In it, organic functions are replaced by mechanical functions. I do not wish to boast, but such an accomplishment is... *revolutionary*."

"It's... astonishing," Sarah said.

"Yes," the Baron said. He went to fill his glass again but the bottle was empty. He put it aside, eyes fixed on some strange infinity. "Having thus succeeded in the gastrointestinal system, I moved on to the others. The skeletal and muscular systems were conquests of the earliest automata. I proceeded to the respiratory and circulatory systems. Each new success encouraged me; each fresh failure but served to spur me on. The nervous system, of course, proved to be the most difficult as well as the most crucial problem. You have seen my first success there."

"The Turk," she said excitedly.

"Yes," he said. "A thinking machine. The day of my success, you cannot imagine my excitement. There remained to enlarge the scope of its capacities. Remember Descartes: passion, memory, imagination. They are all there."

Her head was in a whirl. "So... your machines can do anything a... a living creature can do?"

"Yes, with one exception," he said, a shadow passing over his face. "Reproduction. They cannot reproduce –yet. It is an intensely difficult problem. But I shall solve it." He leaned on the table, his eyes fixed on hers. "Imagine, Sarah: machines that reproduce themselves."

She sat silent for a few moments, imagining indeed. He waited, seemingly expectant. At last, she said, "The idea is... frightening, somehow."

"At the outset, yes, because it is so new."

"But how do you... How does... How are they controlled?"

He nodded, like a teacher to a promising pupil. "That is indeed a problem, but it is only that: a problem to be solved. As you may have surmised, and correctly, a machine capable of passion, memory and imagination will develop its own thought processes –something like its own will, and in a broader sense, its own personality. Any solution necessitates a careful balance."

"So the machines have their own thoughts, and feelings?"

"Once the capacity is there, it is clear that such processes develop, and on an individual and non-duplicative model."

She felt troubled, her thoughts confused. "Then... they're almost human."

"One might say so."

"But if they're even almost human, one doesn't have the right to control them... They should lead their own lives, make their own decisions."

He smiled. "Sarah, your generous feelings do you credit, but here they are misplaced. In the end, they are still machines. They are created so that they might serve some useful purpose."

"Machines, yes," she persisted. "But machines that think and feel."

"They think and feel in order to better do what they are bid."

She shook her head, profoundly disturbed but unable to formulate her thoughts so that she might refute him. He continued: "Thought exists, like electricity and steam. Lightning was feared, but Franklin tamed it, as Patin harnessed steam. I shall do the same, and more, with thought. One pities not the steamship, nor the locomotive, because they work and do the will of man."

"A locomotive doesn't think or feel," she said stubbornly.

"Sarah," he said gently. "These ideas dismay you because they are so new. But you will see: when you become more accustomed to them, they will be less disturbing. We stand on the threshold of a new era, one that will see profound changes take place in the world. I want you to share them with me."

He sat down and took her hand. Already stunned by what she had heard, she sat passively, looking into his face.

"Sarah, I..." His voice became husky. "I want you to marry me. I'll make you a baroness. You will never want for anything. No, don't answer yet."

He seemed to be composing his thoughts. After a moment, he went on: "Sarah, you are alone. Your husband is dead, and now your father. Nothing keeps you in this savage, violent land where you don't belong. We can go away, live in Europe. Switzerland is beautiful. Or if you prefer, we can live in Paris, or Vienna. The choice is up to you. I am a man of means now, but soon we will be very wealthy –so wealthy the mine your father lost will seem negligible."

She frowned, not understanding.

"Come," he said. He took her hand and led her from the room, through a closed set of doors and down an unfamiliar corridor, continuing to discourse as they went. "A European war is coming. A terrible war. The recent war between France and Prussia was but a prelude. The coming war will be far more general, perhaps worldwide. It cannot be avoided. The great nations of Europe will soon find themselves locked in a mortal struggle, their fingers at each other's throats. France, Germany, Russia, England –all will be bled white. None has the advantage." They stopped before another door, which he unlocked with a key from his pocket. "But I can change that."

She looked at him in shock as his meaning dawned on her.

"Yes!" he said, opening the door. They entered his workshop, an astonishing place, filled with tools and machinery, and a thousand bits and pieces of mechanical apparatuses. He pointed toward a squat figure that stood before them. "There is the prototype of a mechanical soldier."

The thing was almost a parody of a human being. Smaller than a man, its head was a flattened sphere, with lenses that served as eyes. From its cylindrical body projected two stubby arms, but its legs were jointed backwards, like the legs of a horse. It had something horrible about it, an inexpressible malevolence.

"A fighting mechanical man," the Baron said with pride. "It knows neither pity nor fear, obeys every order to the letter, and is almost indestructible. Furthermore, the firepower it can deliver is astonishing. No human army could withstand it. I will show you." He led her behind a safety barricade. In one hand he held some kind of controlling apparatus that looked simple enough. He touched a switch and the top half of the thing's torso rotated three hundred and sixty degrees. At the touch of another switch it raised one arm, to point at a large section of log that stood against the wall.

"Do not be alarmed," the Baron said. He touched another switch. Sarah jumped, covering her ears, as rapid gunfire erupted from the upraised arm, the bullets gouging into the wood and showering splinters everywhere. Excruciatingly loud, the burst lasted perhaps ten seconds. When it ended, the log was blasted almost in two, the air filled with the reek of burnt powder.

"The armaments are varied and interchangeable," the Baron said. "That was a rapid-fire small caliber gun, comparable to Gatling's, but much improved. There is the option of cannon fire, thus solid shot, grape, canister, and so forth, and also rockets, that is, self-propelled charges. Highly versatile."

Appalled, Sarah said, "Does it... think?"

"There are deliberate, intentional limits to its intelligence. It is purely a fighting machine. It seeks its target, and kills."

"But... If one side has it, won't the other side develop it, too?"

"Ah!" The Baron smiled. He took her arm and led her from the workshop, locking it behind them. "You are a very astute woman. Yes, given an example –let us say, one lost, or damaged in combat –a counter-weapon might be developed. It would even be possible to deduce its engineering in reverse, and thus construct a copy. But that would take the finest scientific minds, and, what is more important, it would take time. And that time would not be available. Such a weapon shortens war, from months to weeks, or perhaps days. His armies devastated, the enemy would capitulate long before the first steps could be taken."

They were back in the dining room. The Baron led her to her seat. "So you see," he said. "He who possesses such an army will be the master of Europe, perhaps the world. I shall sell these invincible machines to the highest bidder, for they will mean swift and certain victory."

Filled with revulsion, she couldn't even look at him. He squeezed her hand.

"Baron, I..."

"Don't answer now," he said. "Think it over. You have all the time you need."

Someone knocked at the door. The Baron looked up, frowning. "Yes?" he said, irritation in his voice.

A servant entered. Sarah started: she had never seen this man before, yet he might have been James Young's brother. His hair and eyes were different, but the shape of his face, his general size and build, even his approximate age –all were quite similar, remarkably so. But without a look at her, the man approached the Baron, bent over and whispered a few words in his ear. The Baron turned and looked searchingly into the man's face. "Gone?" the Baron repeated with a stunned air. "You're quite sure?" The other man nodded. "Go, and wait for me in the workshop." The man bowed, and left without another word.

"You will excuse me," the Baron said to Sarah. He looked utterly preoccupied, and worried. "An urgent matter..." He got up and hurried away.

She sat there for a few minutes, trying to make sense of it all, to slow the whirl of thoughts in her mind. Marry him – live in Europe –sell his armies of machines to the highest bidder, to wage a great and inevitable war: from anyone else she would have thought it all a poor joke, or worse, the ravings of a diseased brain. From the Baron, it had the air of truth –a monstrous truth. Oh, he had been kind to her, and she cared for him, but the rest? It seemed like madness –but she had seen the machine. And now? Oh, she would herself go mad!

She left the dining room and wandered through the house, aimlessly. There was no one about, and she wondered about the emergency that had called the Baron away. Something to do with the machines, she supposed. She went out into the garden, hoping the night air would do her good.

Outside the air was cool and pleasant, and the odors from the fragrant blossoms lifted her spirits somewhat. She sat for a time, lost in thought, until a rustle of leaves made her look up. It was James. She stood, and he took her in his arms. Trembling, she let him hold her, feeling safe now, she couldn't have said why. After a time, she realized she was crying. "Now, now, Sarah," he said, looking in her eyes, his own so gentle. "You're going to make me think I should have let you be."

"No, James," she said. "It's not you... I don't know why I'm crying."

He made her sit again, and sat beside her with his arm around her. Confused, unsure what to say, but sure it would be indiscreet to mention her talk with the Baron, she explained the steps she thought to take concerning the mine. He listened closely, nodding with approval now and then. When she finished, he said, "I think you are quite right about everything, Sarah, but I wish you would promise me one thing."

"What?"

"That once you have reached San Francisco and found representation, you will stay there, and never return here again."

"But James!"

"No, I mean it." He hesitated, as if what he wanted to say might be painful to her. "Sarah, there's nothing for you here, nothing but danger, maybe even death. You've already been threatened and abused. The next time... What if I weren't there to protect you the next time? There's no telling what they might do. Your legal claim on the mine can be handled from a distance. Leave here, Sarah, leave here and never come back."

She didn't know what to say. "But... the Baron has been so kind..."

"Yes," James said. "The Baron is a generous man." He went, musingly: "But is he... Sarah, do you find him quite *sane*?"

He had said it, had uttered the words; but now she felt ashamed of her own thoughts, loath to hear them uttered aloud. She went on as if he hadn't spoken, saying shyly: "And what of you, James –if I left?"

His face was grave. "I'll miss you, Sarah. I'll miss you very much."

"Couldn't you come with me?"

He shook his head. "No... It's impossible. I must stay here."

"But why?"

"This is my place." He sighed. "I belong here."

She clung to him, crying softly. She had lost everything; was she to lose him, too? At that moment she understood her own heart. The feeling was so strong it came welling up, and she couldn't hold it back. "But James, I... I love you."

He nodded. "Sarah... I love you, too."

He kissed her then, a long slow kiss. The tears dried on her face, and she felt that this, at least, had been worth coming so far, and enduring so much. He held her close in his strong arms and she could feel her own heart beating, strong and sure, telling her everything was alright.

But she heard noises now, back somewhere near the house. At first she ignored them, content in her happiness, but they grew louder: shouts, the barking of dogs. He tensed up and drew away. "What is it?" she said.

"I have to go," he said. "They're..."

"Is someone looking for you?"

"Yes." She was surprised that his face was so grim. "Sarah, listen to me. We may never meet again. You must go away. Remember what I said. Go away and never come back."

He kissed her once again, and then he rose up and was gone, into the dark.

*   *   *

She'd never know how she passed the night. After a time she went back to her room, but in its solitude she found herself crying all over again. Her whole life had become nothing but emptiness and loss...

In the morning she'd cried herself out and she felt calmer, though drained and numb. She knew now that she had to leave, that without James there was nothing more for her here, and that she could no longer go on accepting the Baron's hospitality. Whether she'd ever be back, she didn't know. She sat for a time composing her thoughts, and preparing what she had to say: she cared for the Baron, but she didn't love him, and couldn't marry him; of course he would be disappointed, but she hoped he would understand. Once she'd gone over it enough in her mind, she rose to go downstairs. It was pointless to drag it all out; the situation was already painful enough.

But there she found only Maria, who told her the Baron was out, but could say no more. Sarah sat alone again in the dining room, frustrated in her plans and at a loss. She was drinking a cup of coffee, wondering what to do, when she heard a rider outside, and someone pounded at the entrance door. Maria hurried past, but returned moments later, an anxious look on her face, even as the rider galloped away.

"Señora," Maria said. "A man, he leave this for you." In her hands was a plain envelope, which she reluctantly gave to Sarah.

"Who was it? Did you know him?"

"No, señora. I never see him before."

She went away hesitantly, still looking worried. Sarah waited until the girl was gone to open the envelope. Inside was a single sheet of paper, on which was printed in block letters:

IF YOU WANT TO KNOW WHAT HAPPENED

TO YOUR FATHER, COME TO THE MINE

BUT TELL NO ONE AND COME ALONE

She read and reread the message. Her heart was going hard and she was torn by doubt and conflicting emotions. Who had sent it? What did they know? Why now? Was it someone who wanted to help her –someone perhaps who'd known her father? Or was it but a trap?

She refolded the paper and put it back in the envelope. If only there were someone to whom she might turn, who might help her! But both James and the Baron were gone, and somehow she knew it wouldn't wait.

She went to the window and looked out at nothing, seeing in her mind her father's grave. She heard his words again: 'You have to be self-reliant, my girl. There's no one you can count on but yourself.'

That's how he had lived his life, and that was what he had taught her. And he hadn't been one to back down. She made up her mind, went upstairs and put on her riding clothes. The last thing she did was check the derringer. She didn't consider herself a fool: this had to be done, although it might very well be a trap. But Frank Hayworth's daughter would face it down.

In the kitchen Maria tried to stop her: "No, no! Is not possible! Is no one... to ready the wagon..."

"Fine," Sarah said. "I'll take care of it myself."

"No!" The girl was almost frantic. "The Baron, he..."

Sarah took an imperious tone: "Maria, the message you brought me was urgent! There's no time to lose. I've got to go."

The girl went out wringing her hands. Sarah could almost have laughed: she wasn't used to giving orders, or playing the lady of the manor. But it worked: in a few minutes she heard the wagon coming around.

She went out, still favoring her ankle. The man climbing down was the one who might have been James' brother. Once again, the resemblance was startling: he had James' size and build, and James' face, though James' eyes were blue, and this man's green. But he wore the clothes of a ranch hand, and carried no gun. On his face was a look of confusion and dismay. He opened his mouth to speak.

She didn't wait for him, just climbed up on the seat and took the reins. "Thank you," she said in a pleasant but cool tone. "That will be all." It was something she'd heard the Baron say. She shook the reins and drove off. When she glanced back, just before going out of sight, he was still standing there, with the same consternated look. She smiled to herself at that.

On her first trip to the mine, they'd gone overland, by some trails James knew. Now, in the wagon, she had to go back through town and take the main road. She didn't like it: people there knew her business, and might see her. And she was apprehensive of meeting Blackie and his ilk. But all the way the road was empty, and she met no one.

Coming through town she kept her eyes down and drove along without slowing. She wondered if anyone was watching. Experience had taught her to be distrustful. As she passed the marshal's office, she asked herself if she should stop, let him know what was going on, where she was headed. But the note had explicitly said to tell no one, and she wasn't sure she trusted the marshal anyway. He hadn't done a lot to help her up till now. But once again, as she drove along the dusty street, it struck her how alone she was and she felt newly disquieted, despite her resolve.

But the town fell behind her and she entered the broken country that led to the mine. She saw again the miners working their stakes, heard again the chink of pick and shovel, the periodic detonation. Soon, a huge dust cloud seemed to be rumbling along the road toward her: a mule team, hauling another load of ore from the mine. She pulled off the road to let it pass. The dust was choking, the noise terrific; the teamsters swore at the mules, cracking their whips and wiping dirt and sweat from their faces; behind, the ore wagons trundled along, three of them, huge things, heavily loaded. When they had passed, she shook up the reins and went on, still hearing it long after it had disappeared into its cloud of dust.

Coming over a rise, she saw the mine, not far now. From this direction, most of the buildings were low, hulking. Although no one was around –it had to be the middle of the shift –the same numbing roar made itself heard as before, banging, clanking and clanging, and the same black smoke poured from the boiler house. She slowed up, unsure where to go or how to approach the whole business. As she went by, two lone miners laid aside their shovels and mounted up. She paid them little mind and kept on driving until she heard one call, "Ho! Hey there, ma'am."

She reined up, turned and saw the two men had their pistols drawn, pointed at her. Her heart sank: one of them was Blackie. Almost unrecognizable, his face was mottled purple and yellow with bruises, and he had a rag tied over his head that seemed to be holding his jaw in place. He spoke only by moving his lips; she had some difficulty understanding him.

"Miss Hayworth. Glad you could make it. Drive on. Up to the mine."

Though disquieted, she couldn't help thinking what a wreck he was, just pitiful. "Blackie," she said, looking at the ruin that had been his face. "Haven't you had enough trouble out of all this?"

His words came in little bursts, as though that was all he could manage: "Drive up there. Or I shoot you down. Where you are."

Clearly he meant it. She shrugged and shook up the reins. The whole thing had become somewhat unreal.

They set off. As they rode, he holstered his gun, and took a bottle from his pocket. She saw the label: laudanum. He unscrewed the cap and took a long drink, then another. He had to drink in a peculiar sucking fashion, moving only his lips. It was grotesque. She laughed lightly and said, "Jaw hurting, Blackie?"

"Shut up." He took another long sucking drink, recapped the bottle and put it away. She saw that his pupils were completely dilated from the drug.

"They say that stuff's habit-forming," she said. He didn't answer but his fist tightened on the reins.

They pulled up at a hitching post near the hoisting works. Blackie dismounted and tied up. He motioned for her to get down, and turned to the other man.

"Franklin. Get rid of the wagon. Unhitch the horse. Let it go. Find its own way. Back to town."

Franklin nodded. He got up on the seat, took the reins and drove off. Sarah watched the wagon go. She kept her face impassive but she was worried now. It seemed they intended to make her disappear.

She looked around at the bleak landscape, so filled with noise and yet so empty all around. Was this how it would end? Had she come here to die? She didn't want to –but she was her father's daughter: she'd show them she wasn't afraid. And she still had her gun.

"Get moving," he said, and shoved her. She stumbled, nearly fell.

"You're a beast," she said. "I almost felt sorry for you, but now I see how misplaced that would be."

He just pointed to the hoisting works. His face was vague; she guessed he was numbed by the drug. She turned and strode toward the structure, determined to meet whatever was coming head on. When she got to the door she didn't wait for him, just opened it and went in.

Inside the rumble of machinery intensified but after the blinding sunlight she couldn't see anything at first. She had a strange sense of being just at the mouth of a cavern: echoing sounds seemed to come from far below and the air wafted up a strange scent of dust and rock, foul water and burning oil. A shaft of light poured in as Blackie entered and she saw that another man stood waiting there: the banker Northrop.

"Mr. Northrop," she said, pouring scorn into her voice. "I might have known I would find you here."

He nodded his head. Her eyes were adjusting, and she saw he wore a foreman's coat. Beads of sweat dampened his thinning hair.

"Miss Hayworth," he said. "For once it's a pleasure."

"Not for me. You'll excuse me if I don't give you my hand."

"Of course." He mopped his face with a silk handkerchief, incongruous with his workman's clothes. "Madam, you have been a thorn in my side since your arrival. I tried to discourage you, to prevail upon you to leave, but your stubbornness rivals that of your father. So matters have come to this." He indicated the hoists with one plump hand. "Shall we go down and have a look at the mine?"

She was frightened now, very frightened, but she held her head high and gave him a disdainful look as she walked past him onto the hoist cage. He and Blackie followed her. The gunman threw a lever and the cage lurched; with a clanking of chains, it sank down into the dark. Now she saw a great sparkle of lights, like so many stars, that rose to meet them and passed overhead; and among them, perceived but dimly, a vast wooden structure, formed of box upon box of interlocking timbers. It was like looking into a huge honeycomb. But the banker was talking:

"You see, the main lode runs lengthwise along the face of the mountain. The earliest prospectors were looking for gold, using a rocker on the slope above. They found a small amount but there was a much larger quantity of a heavy blue-black material that clogged the rocker and interfered with washing out the fine gold. When assayed, this turned out to be almost pure sulphuret of silver.

"At first the ore was extracted by surface diggings, but these were quickly exhausted, and it became necessary to tunnel underground. The results on average were poor, and most gave up and moved on. What your father discovered –God knows how, he wouldn't tell –was a massive lode starting over four hundred feet down. Now, most silver ore deposits occur in long thin veins. This lode is more than a hundred feet wide and in some places fifteen hundred feet below the surface. Its estimated value was hundreds of millions of dollars.

"Do you follow me? Hundreds of *millions!* Most ores are considered good grade if the yield is a few hundred dollars per ton of rock. The assay showed here a minimum of forty-five hundred per ton in silver.

"Oh, there are costs! Sometimes as high as seventeen, eighteen dollars a ton. But the yield!"

He stopped the hoist. Sarah felt a touch of vertigo, looking out at this great scaffolding all about her, the timbers as big as a man's body. But the banker was still talking.

"The ore is so soft it can be removed by shovel, but due to the weakness of the rock, cave-ins were frequent. The only possible solution was Deidesheimer's square-set timbering." He gestured with one hand. "As the ore is removed, it's replaced by timbers set in a cube six feet on a side. The ore is progressively replaced by this timber lattice, and the voids re-filled with waste rock."

He took her arm and led her out of the hoist cage, along a sort of passageway where a flooring of planks permitted them to walk along the rails. Now she could hear the chink of shovels, the wheels of the ore cars as they rolled along the tracks, and the voices of men as they called to one another or sang bits of song while they worked. Gears clashed constantly, and in her chest she could feel the throbbing of hydraulic pumps. Ore crashed from wheelbarrows into cars, or onto lifts set at an incline. The place was claustrophobic, the heat almost unbearable. She had trouble getting her breath; wheezing, the banker mopped his head continuously; but Blackie walked as one numbed.

They came to a point where tracks crossed at right angles. The banker took Sarah's arm and led her to the right, following the rails. They seemed to go along a considerable distance; Sarah wondered dully where. She was thinking of the gun. She had two shots; but how to get it out and fire? She had never killed. Could she? Then they squeezed past several cars loaded with waste. The track divided into a turnout; one stub ended in a wheelstop on the edge of a drop-off. She wiped sweat from her eyes. The pit of Hell will be like this, she thought.

"Your father was a stubborn man, Miss Hayworth," Northrop said. He was laboring for breath, the sweat pouring from him. "Too stubborn, like you. He hadn't the funds to exploit this strike. I offered to go into partnership with him, but he only wanted loans for operating capital –his pride, you understand. At first, I complied. But the lode was too valuable –fabulously valuable. And he cared so little for money, you'd have thought him an ascetic!

"I am greedy, Miss Hayworth. It is a fault –a sin, they say. I want to be rich –rich enough to leave this wretched country, and go east, to Boston, perhaps, or New York – somewhere worth living. I need money, more than I can get making loans, and charging interest. Your father brought me here. He wanted another loan. There was an accident. He fell in there." He pointed to the pit. "He's still there."

Confused, Sarah said, "But I saw his grave..."

The banker smiled. "The mine foreman is my man. Anyone will be your man, if you pay them enough. The foreman backed up everything I said. It was all quite in order. And at your father's house, we buried the man who forged those documents that upset you so much."

Outraged, she stared at him, unable to say a word.

"It's all quite tidy," Northrop went on. "Until you arrived, everything was going perfectly. No one expected you. Martinson's letter was just a formality. But you've been a problem. I have to eliminate problems."

"You're a monster."

"That may or may not be true," he replied, "but in any case I've heard all I want to hear from you. Are you ready to join him, Miss Hayworth?"

He turned to Blackie. "Throw her in the pit," he said, "and dump the tailings in after her." He turned to leave. "I'll wait for you at the mine head. I've got another job for you."

He squeezed past the cars loaded with waste and was gone. Blackie turned to Sarah. His dull pinned-out eyes were empty, but he said, "Well, Miss Hayworth. I'd hoped to enjoy. Your feminine charms. Before I killed you. I guess now I. Won't get that chance."

This is it, she thought. Hit him where it hurts... then shoot him.

He stepped toward her. She swung her fist with all her strength at his jaw. Surprised, he caught her wrist just in time, jerked her off balance, and twisted her arm behind her back, hard. She bit off a cry of pain.

"You hell-cat," he whispered. "I ought to…"

He shoved her toward the edge of the pit. She couldn't reach the gun. Below, she glimpsed a deep shaft, the bottom lost in shadow. She struggled, tried to twist away, but his grip was too strong.

"Look at it," he said in her ear. "That hole. Will be your grave."

Tears started from her eyes –but then came the sound of voices behind them, and someone shoved Northrop roughly back past the cars. He stumbled, fell, and scrambled away. Behind him stood James.

"You," Blackie said, as James came for him. He threw Sarah aside and drew his gun, but James struck the outlaw's hand and the gun clattered away and fell into the pit. Blackie swore. He looked around and saw a shovel leaning against the wall. He snatched it up and brandished it before him like a club. "Come on," he said. "Come on!"

James rushed him. Blackie feinted, ducked back as James tried to close, and swung the shovel with both hands. It struck James on the side of the head with a loud *clang!*

"No!" a voice cried in dismay behind them. Sarah turned, as the Baron pushed past the cars of tailings, a look of horror on his face. "No, stop!"

Stunned, James stood shaking his head. Blackie swung the shovel again with all his strength. It banged into James' skull, and Blackie staggered back. James blinked; a convulsion went through him but he stayed on his feet.

"You fool," the Baron whispered.

Blackie swung the shovel again. It smashed into James' head a third time. Sarah couldn't understand: how could he take such terrible blows?

But it had slowed him. He stalked toward Blackie, who backed away, flinching from the hands that reached for his neck, until his shoulders touched the rock wall. Blackie dropped the shovel and clawed at his waist, as James' fingers closed around his throat. Somehow the rag tore loose, and Blackie's jaw fell open. He screamed, a horrible tearing scream –but he pulled a derringer from his belt, brought it up point-blank against James' stomach, and fired both shots. The reports echoed through the mine, loud bangs of metal striking metal, and ricocheting away. The Blackie choked as James' fingers crushed his windpipe, and the little gun dropped from his nerveless hand.

Sarah stood, mouth agape. It was incredible, but at last she understood.

James tossed Blackie's limp body aside. It flopped down on the edge of the pit and fell in. James didn't even look: he turned to Northrop, hands reaching out. The banker cringed away.

"No!" the Baron said. "James, no!"

James blinked and his face twitched but he didn't stop.

"No!" The Baron was shouting now. "I'm ordering you!"

But James no longer seemed to acknowledge the Baron's authority. Instead, he hauled the banker to his feet and hurled him back against the wall. Northrop cowered away, whimpering, "Please... Please..." James took him by the shirtfront and threw him against the wall again. Northrop sank down, mewling, and tried to crawl away. James grabbed him, took his head in both hands and twisted. Sarah shrieked. She heard a *crack!* like a tree limb breaking, and Northrop collapsed in a heap on the mine floor. James looked at him for a moment, then reached down, picked up the body and threw it into the pit.

A shocked silence followed. Sarah was crying quietly, and the Baron stood with his face clenched, hands hanging at his sides. James, too, stood motionless for a long moment, some sort of calm succeeding his brutal rage.

"My God," the Baron said, almost to himself. "How... How will I explain... this?"

"What happened?" Sarah asked. "I don't understand."

"The thinking mechanism," the Baron answered, gesturing vaguely toward James. "It's very delicate. Those blows to the head... It couldn't sustain them."

James looked at him. "That pig the banker deserved to die. He got what was coming to him."

"You disobeyed my order," the Baron said accusingly. "For some time now you've been acting according your own volition. And I tolerated it! I wanted to see you grow, and develop. But this time you disobeyed my direct order."

The gunman shrugged. The light was dim, but somehow his eyes looked all wrong. "My life will be short," he said in a flat dull voice. "It comes to an end like a clock running down, and I know I must die. I never had a childhood, and I'll see no old age. But I will possess this woman." He gestured toward Sarah. "I love her."

Sarah gasped. "Have you lost your mind?" the Baron demanded.

"You gave me feeling," James said bitterly. "Sentiment. Appetites, and needs. Yet I have had so few experiences. A man like me would have already lived thirty years. Thirty years! But I've had only a few months, and now I must die. But not before I possess this woman. I love her."

"Enough of this nonsense!" the Baron said, his voice angry.

A dark look crossed James' face. "You made me this way," he said. "You created me. Any wrong I do... you are responsible for it." He turned to Sarah. "Come to me."

She shrank back. "Enough!" the Baron said.

"Come to me, Sarah." He took a step toward her.

"I forbid this!" the Baron cried.

James ignored him. "Sarah?" he said. His expression was desolate.

Once again tears were running down her face. "James," she said, her voice choked. "I had feelings for you, too. But..." She trailed off, unable to say more.

"But what?" James demanded. "You can't love a machine?"

"That's enough!" the Baron said.

"Stay out of this," James told him. He went to Sarah and took her hands in his. "Sarah, I love you." But she was shaking her head, crying and saying no. "I need you. Don't turn me away." He brought her closer, and kissed her on the lips.

"Let her go!" the Baron raged. He laid hands on the gunman's arm, trying to make him let her go. James shook him off.

"Tell me you love me, Sarah. At least tell me you love me."

"James," she sobbed. "Please..."

"You monster," the Baron said.

The automaton turned toward him, its face a mask of hate. Sarah slipped from his grasp and shied away. "A monster," James repeated. "I like that. You made me, Baron.

You imagined yourself like a god. But she's always preferred me, and now you find yourself jealous of your own creation. A wretched god, Baron!" He laughed spitefully. "A pitiful god, insanely jealous of the very thing he created! Ah, but the Tree of Life has borne bitter fruit!"

Sarah saw in the Baron's face the truth of the automaton's words. She felt choked, couldn't get her breath. "Please!" she sobbed again. But the Baron threw himself at the gunman, his fists battering the automaton's face. "Ha!" James laughed, his own hands taking the Baron's throat. They turned in a circle, grunting and gasping, feet stamping as they pushed and pulled.

"Stop!" Sarah said. "Stop it, both of you! Listen to me!"

They turned about again, muscles straining, each choking the other. James grinned wolfishly as the Baron's face turned red, then purple.

"Stop it, I'm begging you!" Sarah cried.

Boots scraping, they went around again. The Baron's heel hit the steel rail stop and he lost his balance. They tottered on the edge for a sickening moment, locked in a death-grip –then fell. Sarah saw James' eyes, seeking hers, before they disappeared. She screamed, didn't hear the dull crash at the bottom of the pit.

The miners found her there, on her hands and knees, looking over the edge. They couldn't see anything at the bottom, though she made them shine their lights down. She let them lead her away and take her up on the hoisting cage. They wanted to send for a doctor but she just shook her head no, got up on James' horse and rode away. She didn't have any idea where she was going.

Our Lady of Sorrows

i.

King Fairley opened his eyes as the train screeched to a stop and steam blasted from the cylinders. The manacles were chafing his wrists and he rubbed the sore spots absently. After a moment the conductor passed through the car, calling the name of the station. Nobody moved.

Fairley looked around. He hadn't exactly been asleep, but the heat and the swaying of the car had made him groggy, and he'd dozed. The marshal sat slumped next to him, staring straight ahead. Fairley hadn't caught the name of the town, but he didn't care, as long as it wasn't Yuma. There wasn't much to it: beyond the depot on one side he saw a few clap-trap buildings, bleached by the sun; on the other side, nothing but desert. The stop was probably to take on water.

Fairley sat up and stretched his legs. He would have liked to get up, maybe walk up and down the car a little, but he said nothing. The marshal wasn't just real accommodating of his comfort. He stretched his neck and looked out the window, telling himself to relax and enjoy the ride.

Going to Yuma: there wasn't much good you could say about it. Bad luck was what it was. Of course, it had gone worse for the other fellows. He often thought of them: Kyle, the Dutchman, Pistol Pete... That last job had been a mistake. Oh, the payroll money was there, and Pete cracked the safe just as pretty as you please; but the company had hired extra men as insurance, and they were right across the street when the safe blew. The boys were shooting it out before they'd even bagged all the money.

Kyle was standing guard out front and he went down like that, shot full of lead. Pete, the Dutchman and Fairley made it to the horses tethered behind the bank and rode out hell for leather, but the posse was behind them just as soon as they could get in the saddle. An unlucky shot took Fairley's horse and she threw him as she fell. He tried to jump but his foot caught in the stirrup, and he slammed down hard on his shoulder. For a minute he lay there stunned as the posse thundered past; somehow he couldn't even push the dead horse's leg off him. Back at the jail the doc said his collarbone was broken. He felt helpless, could hardly hold a knife or fork. They brought Pete and the Dutchman back on pack horses, shot all to hell, and buried them with Kyle on Boot Hill. A couple of men had been killed during it all. Fairley hadn't done it; he'd never fired a shot. But the others were dead, and King Fairley stood trial, once the judge finally got there. By then the bone was almost healed. The judge told him that was good, and sentenced him to hard labor at Yuma. Fifteen years.

Shouts came along the track, a door banged, the whistle blew, and the train set off again. Fairley watched as the little town fell behind and there was nothing but desert. He settled back on his seat. This was his first train ride, and something said to him it would be his last. Fifteen years labor at Yuma –that was pretty much a death sentence, however you looked at it.

For a time he looked out the window but the view was monotonous, and after a while he dozed again. A sudden lurch awoke him. He sat up and looked around. As far as he could see there wasn't a station in sight, but the train was slowing down fast. The marshal's mouth was tight.

As the train came to a stop, brakes complaining and the wheels squealing on the rails, they heard gunfire. The few other passengers looked worried. The marshal stood up: "You stay put, you hear?" He drew his gun and moved along the aisle to the door.

Outside Fairley heard more shots and voices shouting. A man on horseback went past. Fairley stood up and looked cautiously out the window. Several mounted men, armed with rifles, were reined up near the locomotive. Beyond them he could see some kind of barricade across the track. One of the crew clambered down from the tender and trudged back to a boxcar, followed by two of the bandits. The crewman took out a ring of keys and fitted one to the boxcar's lock. Fairley couldn't see the marshal.

As the crewman fumbled nervously with the key, a shot rang out. The men on horseback wheeled around and spurred their mounts. The crewman turned and hurried toward the front of the train. Another man, probably the engineer, swung down behind him and they began to clear the track. On the other side of the train Fairley heard shots. A window shattered as a volley slammed into the passenger car. Fairley ducked down, saw the others already on the floor.

He squeezed out into the aisle, hampered by the manacles, and duck-walked toward the front of the car, staying below the level of the windows. The shooting had stopped and he heard voices again, but indistinctly. He decided to chance it and rose up to look out the window. Now the engineer was standing with his hands over his head while the other crewman opened the boxcar at gunpoint. The door slid open with a bang and one of the armed men climbed up and in.

Fairley caught movement in the corner of one eye: one of the bandits, circling the train, and watching for trouble. He had his rifle across one arm, ready. Fairley flattened against the side of the car and froze.

He didn't have much time. When the rider passed out of sight, Fairley turned and opened the door to the vestibule. The marshal was there, crumpled in one corner. He'd been hit several times. Blood was pooling on the steps and more was splattered on the vestibule walls.

Fairley picked up the marshal's gun, opening it awkwardly. The marshal had gotten off three shots. Fairley ejected the empty casings, reloaded and stuck it down his waistband, pulling his shirt over it. Stooping, he went through the marshal's pockets until he found the key to the manacles.

The things were cleverly made: even with the key, they were almost impossible to get off. Fairley was struggling unsuccessfully with them when a voice said, "Well, what do we have here?"

He looked up and saw one of the gunmen, a tall man whose face was seamed on one cheek with a long scar. He had an empty sack in one hand, and a Colt in the other. Fairley said nothing.

"So this is the hero who opened up on us," the tall man said. "Well! A marshal... You his prisoner?"

"Yep," Fairley said. "He was taking me to Yuma."

"Yuma," the man repeated, and spit on the floor as if the word left a bad taste in his mouth. "Well, this here just might be your lucky day." He looked through the window at the passengers. "You stay right here," he said. "I got some business to tend to."

He raised one foot, kicked open the door, and fired the Colt. Glass shattered and a woman cried out.

"Listen to me!" he shouted, going through the door. "One man is already dead. Don't be like him. Sit tight and do as you're told and I give you my word none of you will be harmed. But I'll shoot the first one who gives me any trouble.

"Ladies! I want your jewelry, rings, watches, any money you have. Gentlemen, your wallets and pocket watches –but nice and slow, if you want to keep on living."

He went through the car, collecting everything of value. No one gave him any trouble. In moments he was back. "Alright, you," he said to Fairley. "Come with me."

They got down from the train, the tall man first, Fairley following. The tall man whistled and waved to one of the others. "Hey, Romeo," he called. "Look a-here."

The other man rode up, looking at Fairley suspiciously. He wore a battered sombrero and a short riding jacket with fancy embroidery, and he was riding a mustang, one of those the vaqueros called a grulla. His dark eyes weren't friendly. "You have it?" he demanded.

"We got it," the tall man answered.

"Who's this?"

"The man we killed was a marshal," the tall man told him. "This one says he was taking him to Yuma."

"No bueno," the Mexican said. "Kill one lawman, the others don't rest till they get you." He looked around and spit. "We should kill them all, burn the train."

"Romeo, wait a minute," the tall man said. "Then it's murder, and we hang if they catch us. But with him..." He looked at Fairley. "Why, it's perfect."

"What's perfect?" Romeo demanded.

"*He* killed the marshal, when he escaped," the tall man said. "See, he's even got the marshal's gun." He pulled up Fairley's shirt, revealing the Colt. He yanked it free, ejected the shells and put them in a pocket, and handed the gun negligently back to Fairley. Romeo nodded, but his eyes narrowed. "What about the passengers?"

The tall man laughed. "They were all under the seats. Look: ten to one the marshal's got the papers in his pocket. If he's dead and sonny boy here is gone, why, the conclusion is obvious. And all we done is rob the train."

"Muy bien." Romeo looked at Fairley, grinning. "You no should kill a lawman, hey? No bueno. Better get moving."

Infuriated by this talk of framing him for something he didn't do, Fairley clenched his fists and glared into the bandit's eyes. "You can't pin this on me, you sorry Mex..."

Romeo clicked back the hammer on his .44. He wasn't grinning now. "Hey, gringo," he said. "Maybe you don't understand. We doing you a favor. We letting you go. No more Yuma! Now, if you smart, you get away, and killing the marshal don't bother you much. If not..." He looked around at the desert, the rails stretching away out of sight, and shrugged. "Eh, vaya con Dios. Now get moving."

Fairley just stood there, looking up at the bandit's face. He wanted to remember it –remember it perfectly, so he'd never forget.

Romeo sneered. "Hey gringo, I no tell you again. But maybe I give you a little nudge."

He fired the .44 almost carelessly. Fairley didn't move. The bullet kicked up sand an inch from his foot.

"That's all right, you damned greaser," Fairley said. "The next time I see you, I won't have *these* to slow me down." He raised his manacled hands.

Eyes cold, the Mexican drew aim at Fairley's chest. But behind him came a blast of steam; the locomotive's wheels slipped, caught; the train began to roll away, picking up speed as it went. Romeo glanced at it, and once more a grin spread across his face. "Hey gringo, I think you miss your train. Is going to be a very thirsty day."

He wheeled his horse about and fired the gun in the air. "Vámonos!" he shouted. "Andale!"

The other bandits spurred their horses and followed him. In a couple of minutes both they and the train were gone.

ii.

Hours later, the sun blazed down from a blinding sky.

He was a dead man. He wasn't going to kid himself. There wasn't any use. Things were better if you looked them square in the eye.

It had to be mid-afternoon. They'd eaten that morning, him and the marshal. He hadn't had so much as a mouthful of water since.

The desert stretched away in every direction. He'd left the rail line behind, knowing any pursuit would come back along it. If they caught him –an escaped convict, whether or not they knew about the marshal –he doubted they'd bother with another trial; they'd just hang him. True, they'd have to take him to a town to do it. Nothing out here grew tall enough.

So he struck north, for lack of a better idea. Now, his eyes almost closed, baking in the oven-like sun, he just kept putting one foot in front of the other. The manacles felt as hot as if newly forged. His tongue was swollen, his lips cracked, and dried sweat itched on his skin. Mostly he had no way to scratch it. Once he tried again to get the manacles off, but he might as well have saved himself the trouble.

He kept walking. If he sat down to rest he'd never get up. But he wouldn't let himself think of the heat, or his thirst.

He kept his thoughts narrowed to a single focus: the Mexican – Romeo. Hate gave him strength.

Not that he'd ever see the bastard again.

For a second, he thought he saw movement, off to one side. He stopped, and holding his hands up to shade his eyes, he squinted against the blinding light, trying to see. But there was nothing there, just sand and rock, cactus and cholla, stretching away to infinity. He shook his head a little, to rid himself of the impression. It must have been his imagination.

Again he made himself move. He'd been heading toward a broad mesa on the horizon. In between it and him was a long broken ridge of dull red rock shoving up through the sand. He knew that such ridges sometimes had a 'tank' hollowed in the rock that collected water, holding it for days, even weeks. That was his only chance: he had to have water – soon –or die.

He trudged heavily forward, trying to measure out his strength. For a time he became prey to awful fantasies of water –cool, fresh water, ladles and gourds full, or little streams where he could stretch out on the green grass and drink his fill. His mind tortured him with ever-shifting scenes of water, and he couldn't make it stop.

He tripped, recovered, but felt himself swaying, as if he might fall over. The rock ridge looked just as far off as it had before. He pushed on, strength fading. A grim acceptance settled over him. This was a bad place to die, but you didn't always get to pick. He'd wanted to start over, go to California and start a new life. Robbing and stealing hadn't set well with him. Maybe that was his upbringing... He'd thought to pull one last job, take his share and get out. Well, it hadn't worked out that way. Now he guessed he was reaping what he'd sown, for it looked like he would die here.

The ridge –get to the ridge.

But it looked further away than ever. He tried not to think, just kept putting one foot in front of another, but the ridge was too far, he no longer believed he could make it. If only there were a bit of shade, somewhere he could lie down and rest, just for a moment.

He stumbled, realized his eyes had closed and he'd almost collapsed. He rubbed dry hands over his face and went on. Fatigue came on again, overwhelming; he couldn't keep going... He fell, and lay in the hot sand.

When he came to again, he began to crawl. His own tongue choked him; his eyes were so blurred he could barely see. He knew he couldn't last much longer. The ridge was ahead, at the top of a long slope. He paused, pulling himself together, and forced himself to his feet. Getting to that ridge was going to take everything he had, and more.

Heart thudding, lungs seared by the baking air, he trudged on. The terrain sloped upward toward the ridge, steeper than he'd thought. A pain like a knife blade sawed at his ribs. He gasped for breath –stumbled, and fell to his knees –got up again, reeling, and went on. Almost there...

A scorpion scuttled across his path. He kicked at it, dully angry that it could live in this arid Hell; but it vanished. Had it even been there at all? Despair settled over him like a physical weight. He was dying, and he knew it.

Somehow he reached the top of the ridge. Blear-eyed, he staggered along the crest till he saw what he was looking for –a tank –and sank down beside it, reaching in a hand, further, further...

The tank was dry. No! –his fingers touched moisture. He gathered what he could, brought it to his lips... Just a taste, that was all.

Somewhere a bell began to toll. It rang for him, tolling his death. He didn't mind. He got up, the sound filling his skull; and now he saw that he stood at the edge of a cemetery. The crude markers, bleached dull grey by the sun, stretched away before him; beyond, not far off, stood a Spanish church, adobe tower lifting toward the sky.

The bell was still tolling, ringing clearly through the hot dry air. It welcomed him, for he had come here to die. For a moment he thought of his mother: she would never know. He hated to pain her.

Everything went black. He crumpled and fell.

iii.

Later, he had vague memories of her. If he thought about them too hard, or tried to remember, it just made his head hurt. There'd been a woman... hadn't there? Was it his mother? He didn't want his mother to know, about Yuma... But no, it wasn't his mother, grey-haired and tired. The woman was young, her hair black... She never spoke, but bathed his face with cool water. Her touch was gentle, and her presence comforted him. Then she was gone. Who was she?

He woke up in bed in a cool dark room, had no idea where he was. The sun filtered past dark shutters. Somewhere a bell was tolling. He wondered about that, vaguely. He looked around. The room, almost bare, held only a table, a chair and a washstand with basin and pitcher. The walls were whitewashed plaster, and on the one opposite the bed hung a crucifix, carved from dark wood.

He tried to sit up but the effort brought a rush of blood to his head. Pain stabbed through his temples and he felt nauseous. He fought it down and swung his feet off the bed, slowly bringing himself upright.

The bell fell silent; all was quiet. His mind felt numb, as if his brain had gone soft. He looked dully around, trying to imagine where he was, and how he had come here. Gradually some of it came back: the train, the robbery, the desert... He looked down at his hands: the manacles were gone, and his wrists, chafed and scratched by the iron, had already begun to heal. How long had he been here? His boots stood neatly against the wall. The marshal's Colt was gone. Someone had brought him here and put him to bed –but who? And why?

As he thought it over, unsure what to do, the door opened and a man entered, carrying a tray. He was dressed in the shapeless white clothes of a Mexican peasant, but from his face he was half Indian. He walked with a stooped, shuffling gait, and a large hump protruded from one shoulder. As he looked at Fairley no expression crossed his face. One of his eyes was blind, just an off-white orb like a boiled egg. On the tray was a platter of food, steaming hot. He put it on the table and turned to go without a word.

Fairley knew a little Spanish. "Hola," he said, and the hunchback turned back. Fairley pointed to the food. "Gracias. Quién es usted?"

"Me llamo Juan-Bautista," the hunchback said.

"Fairley." He looked around, and raised his hands in a questioning gesture. "Dónde estoy?"

"A la sagrada Mission de Nuestra Señora de los Dolores." He turned away again.

"Wait!" Fairley said. "What... How did I get here?" But the hunchback just shook his head and went out the door, closing it behind him.

A mission... What was a mission doing here, so far from anywhere? He remembered the church he'd seen, with its tower, and the graveyard. The padres must have found him.

The smell of the food made him realize how hungry he was. He got up, shaky, and went to the table. The platter was heaped with seasoned beef, tortillas and frijoles. He sat down and began to eat, slowly at first, and then like a starved dog. When he could eat no more he felt better but exhausted. He was still weak. It struck him that he was lucky to be alive. He went back to the bed and lay down.

When he awoke again, the bell was tolling once more. From the fading light, night was falling, and he guessed the bell announced services; the padres would be about their evening prayers. He sat up, feeling better than before, but terribly thirsty. There was water in the pitcher and he drank his fill, then went to the window, opening the shutters. A heavy cast-iron grille barred the window. Beyond, the sun was setting, casting long shadows, but he could see the dead trunks of what had once been an orchard. The rock and sand of the desert came right up to the mission walls.

He turned away, puzzled. The mission was awfully quiet –almost lifeless. He didn't know much about such places, but it seemed strange. What if he explored a little bit? Though everyone was probably in church, he could still look around. But with his hand on the door, he stopped, suddenly apprehensive. Was he free to move about? When they found him, he'd been shackled, and carrying a gun. Was he their prisoner? Were they only holding him until they could hand him over to the law?

With an effort, he shook it off. Surely these were men of God; they would hardly keep him here by force... He would take it as it came.

The door opened on an interior corridor, dark and cool. Doors lined it in either direction, and at one end he saw a courtyard. He turned that way. The bell tolled again, louder now.

None of the doors were open. He passed one after another, wondering what lay behind them. Had it not been for the bell, the place would have been completely silent. The corridor ended at an arcade that surrounded the courtyard. Fairley stopped, looking around curiously.

A breeze was blowing, bringing the sudden cool of night. Dust and sand blew across the packed arid earth of the courtyard. Nothing grew there. A dry fountain stood in the middle, scoured by the wind. Fairley saw now with surprise that the mission was dilapidated and fallen into disrepair; the stucco had flaked away from the walls in great patches, revealing the adobe beneath, and in spots the tile roof had fallen and lay in heaps of broken fragments on the ground. The stalls and workshops of the arcade were empty and cave-like. It must have been years since the mission had been active and full of life. Now it resembled a ghost town.

Fairley's skin prickled a little at this abandon and desolation. What sort of padres lived here, and why?

The bell tolled out again. As it died away, a door opened and shut in the corridor behind him. Fairley turned. From out of the darkness hurried a man.

Of medium height, he wore the dark and shapeless cassock of a monk. Around his waist, a thin knotted rope served as a belt. Its ends fell almost to his feet, shod in buckled shoes of antique design. His black hair, not long, was going grey, as was his thick beard, and his face was lined and tanned by the desert sun. He seemed preoccupied, or burdened with worry; but he started, surprised, when he saw Fairley. A shadow crossed his face. Looking away, he turned the corner and hurried on.

"Wait!" Fairley called. "Padre! A word with you."

Reluctantly the man stopped and turned. "Sí?"

"Padre, I... I owe you people some thanks," Fairley said.

"Give thanks to God. We are only His instruments." The monk crossed himself.

"Yes," Fairley said. He felt awkward, unsure what he was trying to say or learn. "Of course. But... where am I?"

"The holy mission of Our Lady of Sorrows." The monk's eyes shifted nervously.

"Yes, but... the mission..." Fairley began.

"I must away to vespers," the monk said firmly. "I am already late. Father Xavier, the superior of the mission, will answer all of your questions in good time, I am sure. Vaya con Dios!" He turned, and hurried away.

Fairley watched him disappear into the shadows. Was it only his imagination, or was the man afraid of something? But what?

He shrugged. Perhaps it concerned their discipline. He would wait. He seemed to be their guest –that was what mattered. The manacles were gone.

The stars came out, the moon rising. The cool night air was pleasant, but the ghostly silence was oppressive, and he decided to return to his room. As he turned back down the corridor, he heard a door close quietly.

Well, somebody's keeping an eye on me, he thought.

iv.

Fairley was stretched out on the bed resting when the hunchback came to tell him that he would dine with the head of the mission in half an hour. He washed up a little in the basin, combed his hair as well as he could with no mirror and felt of the beard on his face and chin. The last time he'd shaved was back at the jail before he saw the judge –for all the good it had done! Now, well, there was no helping it. When he finished he found Juan-Bautista waiting in the corridor. The twisted little man –a head and a half shorter than him –turned and led the way without a word, and Fairley followed.

They turned into the arcade, the hunchback's lamp throwing shifting shadows as they went. Even by the dim light, Fairley could see the cracked and broken masonry, the heaps of shattered tiles. They turned into another hallway, and there stopped before a door. The hunchback gestured that he should go in.

He found himself in the refectory. One of the tables was set for four, with candles burning. As in his room, the walls were whitewashed, a crucifix hanging on one wall. Fairley stood to one side, waiting.

He didn't have to wait long. The door opened and a tall man entered, clad in the same black cassock and buckled shoes as the first monk. He was older, perhaps fifty or more, but he had a hawk-like air of strength and alertness. Fairley had never seen a man like him. His face, deeply-tanned, suggested nobility: the nose was sharp and strong, a keen intelligence and penetration flashed in his eyes, and in the lines of his mouth was authority, the habit of being obeyed. Yet he smiled warmly and took Fairley's hands in a powerful grip.

"Bienvenido," he said, "in the name of our Lord and Savior Jesus Christ." He bid Fairley sit down and clapped his hands. The hunchback entered with a bottle of wine. The monk took it and poured two glasses.

"Amontillado wine, from Spain. To your health, señor." He threw the glass back. Fairley did the same, and a pleasing warmth began to suffuse him.

"Ah," the monk said. "Muy bien. Señor, I am Father Xavier, lecturer and superior of this mission dedicated to Nostra Señora de los Dolores. I welcome you as our guest."

"Thank you, padre," Fairley said simply.

Xavier asked after Fairley's health. Fairley assured him he was fine, and that he was recovering well.

"Bien," Xavier said. "May God be praised. You know, my son, you are most fortunate that we found you. Had we not, you would have died in the desert."

"Perhaps the good Lord was looking after me," Fairley said. "But I have you to thank for saving my life."

Father Xavier nodded. "The mission is dedicated to the service of God," he said piously, crossing himself. "If you are alive, and safe, it is His doing. Give thanks to Him." He clapped his hands. The hunchback entered again.

"Juan-Bautista!" he said, his tone commanding. "We dine soon. Summon Father Alfonso and the lady Isabella." The hunchback bowed and went away in silence.

When the door opened again, another monk entered, dressed alike in cassock and buckle shoes. He was not as tall, but heavier; his jowls drooped a bit, and his lips were full and fleshy, as if he much relished the pleasures of the table; but his small eyes were keen, and malicious. He was florid, as if he'd just taken strong drink. Father Xavier gave him a look Fairley could not judge, even as he made introductions: this was Father Alfonso, his brother in Christ, a fellow scholar and after him the most senior and responsible of the monks; and his niece, the daughter of his late sister, the lady Isabella. Alfonso nodded to Fairley and went to his seat. Behind him was the most beautiful girl Fairley had ever seen.

She was slender and supple, neither tall nor petite, but of medium height. Heavy black hair fell over her shoulders and down her back. She wore a filmy lace veil over her face, but Fairley saw her large dark eyes, a strong nose, a broad and sensuous mouth. Her expression was serious and reserved, almost regal, and her fine skin was as pale as if she never went out in the sun. Her black silk dress was so simple it might have been severe but for its rich brocade. Fairley was struck almost dumb. He returned the monk's nod; unsure what to do, he bowed a little to the girl. She seemed to smile to herself as she passed. But Xavier was looking at him.

"My name's Fairley," he replied. "Folks call me King but I reckon you should call me Chet, short for Chester." At this he blushed, unsure what more to do or say, and confused by the presence of such a beautiful girl. Strangely, there was something familiar about her...

"Sit down, sit down," Father Xavier was saying. "Let us have some wine. Juan-Bautista will serve the dinner shortly."

"So, my young friend," Father Alfonso said when their glasses were filled. "Your appearance has overwhelmed me with curiosity. How came you to this lonely and isolated place?"

He drank off his wine and regarded Fairley, a penetrating look in his eyes. Fairley hesitated. None of them had mentioned either the manacles or the gun, but certainly no one had forgotten. "I was on the train to Yuma," he said evenly. "There was a hold-up."

"Many valuable things are carried on the train," Alfonso said, smiling to himself, as if at some pleasantry only he understood. "What a pity should they fall into the wrong hands."

"Father Alfonso..." Xavier began, but Alfonso said to Fairley: "Had you business in Yuma?"

"Yes," Fairley said. "A serious matter. But now it's too late." He paused, and began again: "Bandits stopped the train. They must have wanted something in the freight. There was a marshal on board. When he tried to stop them, they killed him."

"A marshal," Alfonso said. "How unfortunate."

I'm not fooling him, Fairley thought. "I was unarmed at the time, so I took the marshal's gun. Once they got what they wanted, they robbed the passengers. I would have stopped them... But it wasn't possible. They put me off the train and sent it on." That didn't completely make sense, he thought.

Juan-Bautista entered bearing a tray, and set about serving the dinner. The others began to eat, and Fairley followed their example. But Alfonso was watching him, clearly

184

enjoying his interrogation. "The rail line is some distance from here," he observed. "The country is inhospitable, to say the least. Why did you not wait for another train, or follow the tracks?"

"I had no idea when there might be another train, or how far a town might be, in either direction," Fairley said. "And I needed water badly –I knew I'd die without it. From the lay of the land I thought I might find some to the north. It seemed my only hope at the time. But there was no water. I woke up here." He looked from one to another of them. "I want to thank you all," he said. "You saved my life. I would have died out there."

"To give succor to those in need is a tenet of our faith," Father Xavier said.

"Indeed," Alfonso said. Fairley could not read his expression, but he saw Xavier give him a look. Alfonso seemed to pay little mind; he poured himself more wine.

Isabella had not spoken until then, but now in a soft, musical voice, she said, "Praised be God that you were saved. You have suffered much." Her eyes were so gentle and kind, her expression so caring and sweet, that he was touched to the core; his heart went out to her. Suddenly, it hit him: she was the woman who had cared for him in his delirium. He wanted to say something, to thank her somehow. Their eyes held for a long moment. He flushed a little, embarrassed and unsure of himself.

"Thank you, señorita," he said, and added, "Praised be God."

"Praised be God," Alfonso repeated, an ironic look on his face. "We have so few visitors here, it would be a shame were one of them to meet an untimely end."

Xavier's eyes narrowed. They ate in silence for a time. Fairley, awkward before them all now, found little to say. Xavier seemed irritated but distracted. Alfonso, pushing his plate aside, helped himself to more wine; he sat, glass in hand, giving Fairley an appraising look, a satisfied expression on his face. Fairley found it unnerving. The girl ate slowly and daintily, with little appetite. Once he glanced up and found her gazing at him, but she dropped her eyes and seemed to blush a little. Curious about me? –but she must know I'm an outlaw, Fairley thought. An outlaw and a convict. He felt abashed, unworthy of her kindness. The other two knew it, for sure. They were discreet, that's all –or was there more? What was their play?

Uncannily, as the plates were being cleared away, Alfonso said, "We would have great difficulty just now helping you to your destination. But in a few days we expect supplies by train, and so we will take the wagon to the nearest station. If you wish, we could see to it that you meet the train to Yuma. But perhaps you would prefer to stay?"

"That's very considerate," Fairley said. He sensed the monk wanted to keep him on edge, and worried –but why?

"Father Alfonso, we must see to our work," Xavier said. He looked displeased. "Will you see Isabella to her room? I will join you shortly."

"Of course," Alfonso said unctuously.

They rose, and Fairley did the same. He nodded to Alfonso, and bowed to the girl. She held out her hand; he took it and brought it to his lips. Father Xavier watched them go with a curious expression on his face.

Fairley expected to be dismissed. Instead, Xavier clapped his hands and bid the hunchback bring more wine.

When it came he took Fairley by the shoulder in a friendly way and urged him to sit. The strength of his hand was impressive. "My young friend, I hope you will indulge an old man who does not wish to sit at table alone."

"The pleasure is mine, padre."

"Ha! Gallantly spoken. Señor Fairley, you are like a fresh wind, blowing from some other clime. I have spent a long time, many years, amidst these walls, and I grow weary."

"How did you come here?" Fairley asked, curious.

The monk tossed down the glass of heady wine. "I came to California as a boy," he said, "as a brother of the Society of Jesus, the order known as the Jesuits. I was something of a prodigy, having mastered Latin by the age of five, and become Doctor of Theology by eleven. Had I stayed in Spain, I should have led a life of scholarship and ecclesiastical honor. But my spiritual father and protector longed to come to the New World, and I begged him to bring me along.

"When we arrived in San Francisco, I found we were outcasts –pariahs –unwelcome in the missions and the houses of God. A hundred years before, our order had been abolished from Alta California and replaced by Franciscan weaklings –for the Crown found them more tractable, and easier to govern.

"The Franciscans lorded it over us, refusing us succor and driving us from their doors, sometimes at most giving us a bit of moldy bread. I saw how my master suffered, and I learned to hate. Our order had carved a land from the wilderness! –and these fools, grown fat and lazy on Indian labor, disdained and despised us. We lived in the streets, slept in stables and barns, begged in the marketplace.

"How I missed Spain –the warm sun, the fine weather! My master was no longer young, and he was from Mallorca. He fell ill... He never uttered a word of complaint but it took his strength. San Francisco can be cold, especially at night. He was a scholar, unused to privation... There he developed the cough. I was young, and ignorant; I thought little of it. By the time I realized he had consumption, he was dying.

"I went to the Franciscans and begged... I humbled myself, crawled on my belly, pleaded... Finally, to rid themselves of me, they gave me fifty dollars and told me never to return.

"We took the stage east, for the Arizona Territory. The dry air helped him, but it was too late. By the time we found this place, he was a walking skeleton. I cooked his food, nursed him... He knew he was dying, so he initiated me into... his work. Had I but learned more! But time was short. When he died, I buried him with my own hands, in the cemetery here. There had not been a fresh grave in almost a hundred and fifty years.

"His work... I carried it on. It takes money. I went back to San Francisco. My sister had settled there, married to a wealthy shipbuilder. She helped me... and in time I found others to help me, with their fortunes, or their skill. And so the great work went on, until now, when I stand on the verge of success!"

His eyes were blazing. Was it the wine, or something else? Unsure what to think, Fairley said, "What is this work, Father?"

"The work?" Xavier said. "The *great* work... I have labored long, but success is almost in my grasp. I have failed so many times... A lesser man would have given up in despair. But I *shall* succeed... at last!"

Fairley was taken back as the monk took something from his cassock and set it on the table: a bullet. Xavier indicated it with one hand. "Do you have much experience with such as this?" he asked.

Fairley saw little point in playing innocent. "Well, yes... Quite a bit."

"Has it brought you much wealth?"

"No." Fairley grinned. "Or anyway, I don't have much to show now."

"What is it made of?"

"Why... Lead, of course."

"Exactly." The padre picked it up, turned it over in his hand. "Common lead. A base substance, of little value." He put it away. "When I succeed –and I *shall* succeed –I will be able to transmute it into gold, the purest gold."

A knock came at the door. "Yes?" Xavier thundered, obviously irritated by the interruption. Juan-Bautista entered.

"What is it?" Xavier demanded.

The hunchback cowered, but went to his master's ear, muttering rapidly.

"I see." Xavier frowned. "Bien. I will be there directly."

Bowing repeatedly, the hunchback went out.

"Señor Fairley," Xavier said, rising. "There is a matter that requires my attention. You will excuse me. Juan-Bautista will show you to your room." He clapped his hands. Fairley bowed a little to his host, and followed the hunchback away.

V.

Juan-Bautista lit the lamp in Fairley's room, made a sort of scraping bow that somehow seemed half mocking, and left again. Fairley heard the key turn in the door. He tried it: locked. He swore a little and looked around, but it was no good. A heavy cast-iron grill secured the window. He was a prisoner.

He stretched out on the bed and stared up at the ceiling. The night was quiet, the cool air that came from the window pleasant. He told himself to relax. Their precautions were natural, after all: they knew nothing of him, save that they'd found him in the desert, manacled and on the run. The wily Father Alfonso had already guessed the truth, and Father Xavier's kindness and piety in no way implied a lack of acumen. Fairley was a convict and a wanted man, and of course, they had the girl to think about.

At the thought of her a sort of restlessness took hold of him. He got up and went to the window. The night was clear and beautiful, a great waxing moon rising over the range of mountains and washing the landscape with pale light. Somewhere a coyote howled. Fairley had never met a girl like Isabella. It was more than her beauty. Her grace and bearing, the gentleness of her words, her tender expression –everything about her said she was more than a lady, that she was something noble and rare. What was more, he was sure she was the one who had taken care of him, in the beginning. When he thought of her, he felt ashamed of himself, of the things he had done and how he had spent his life. She disturbed him; he felt undeserving of her kindness.

This wasn't the first time he'd come to regret his ways. He certainly hadn't been brought up to be an outlaw. His ma had raised him and his brother, younger by two years, after their pa was killed over a card game. And she was strict: no drinking or cussing, and church Wednesday night and twice on Sunday. He hadn't much cottoned to it, and after his own kid brother started talking about becoming a parson, one day he just lit out. He'd worked for a while –helping in a tar camp, and laying rails –and then he fell in with a tough lot; and since he was fast with a gun and scared of nothing, one thing led to another... Now, at twenty-three, he was an outlaw and worse, a convict. He hoped his ma never found out; she'd just die of shame.

His eyes came to rest on a low ridge not far away. Disturbed by the girl and his own memories, it took him some time to recognize the cemetery –where they'd found him. The crude crosses, some upright and straight, and others crazily askew, threw strange shadows on the broken ground. He wondered how many souls had lived and died here, for the mission had to be hundreds of years old. Once there had been cooks, bakers, hostlers, blacksmiths... Now, he'd seen three monks, the hunchback and the girl. How did they live? And what kept them in this place, almost abandoned and in ruins?

Xavier had his work –whatever that was. And perhaps their duty bound them there. The thought gave him a funny feeling. These were men of God; this was their place. Fairley was not a religious man. He'd not been to church since he was a boy. Preaching about sin and Hell –that was for his ma, and his kid brother. But here, in this harsh and lonely place, he had to respect the monks' piety and devotion. That sort of thing wasn't for him, but he had to respect it.

Someone knocked lightly at the door, and a key turned in the lock. He waited, wondering what now. When it opened, to his surprise, he saw the first monk, the one to whom he'd spoken earlier that evening.

The monk made a sign for him to be silent. Furtively, he looked back into the corridor, before closing the door and locking it behind him. He drew Fairley toward the window.

"We must keep quiet," he said lowly. "They must not know I am here."

Fairley nodded, wondering.

"You ask yourself why I have come," the monk went on. "I cannot explain much, for I am bound by the most frightful oaths. But my soul is sickened and my heart rebels. I have come to help you. You must leave this place at once!"

Fairley was taken back. "But why, padre?"

"You have met the lady Isabella?"

"Yes."

"Her life –her very soul –are in mortal danger. Only you can save her."

"Only me! But why? In danger from what?"

The monk didn't answer. He was looking back at the door, listening for something. Fear twisted his mouth. Fairley waited, unsure what this was all about.

"The hunchback spies on me, I am sure of it," the monk said, almost to himself. "Yet he knows not what he risks.

Had I half a chance... I'd break his twisted neck. God forgive me!"

"Padre, I don't understand," Fairley said in a low voice.

The monk looked back at him, his eyes like a cornered beast's. "You must take her away from here. Both of you are in danger. If you stay, your death will be frightful, and she... her eternal soul will be condemned to Hell."

Is he mad? Fairley thought, searching for something to say.

"You do not believe me," the monk said. "Perhaps you think I have lost my reason. Tell me: do you know how you came to be here? Or why you are still alive at all?"

"No... I don't know," Fairley said.

For a long moment the monk said nothing. Jaw clenched, he strained to listen, as if, by force of will, he might hear through the wall. At last, he said, "Isabella found you, in the cemetery. She'd gone there to visit her mother's grave. You were almost dead. She had the hunchback bring you here, and put you to bed. For a week she nursed you back to health."

Fairley nodded; he'd thought so.

"Do you see? You owe her your life! And Xavier tolerates you because it keeps her distracted while he makes his preparations... for the full moon!"

"The full moon," Fairley repeated. What fool talk was this?

"The night of the blood ritual," the monk whispered, his eyes insane. "After that, he will have no further need for you. And they have many dreadful ways... to make a man die!"

"Padre, I..." Fairley began, but the monk cut him off.

"Even if you care nothing for your own safety, think of her! You have no idea what he plans."

"Xavier? But he's her uncle... He was so cordial, and considerate."

The monk's expression twisted in rage: "That smiling face is the mask of a fiend! His piety is a blasphemy, for his infamy rivals that of the demon. He will stop at nothing to fulfill his ambition. He's a monster –a devil!"

Fairley must have looked surprised. The monk made a visible effort to master himself.

"You must take her away from here," he said. "If you do not, no one and nothing can help either of you. I cannot say more –I am sworn to silence by Lucifer himself!"

"Padre," Fairley said. "How can we leave? We're in the middle of the desert. The girl would die out there..."

"Tonight I can do nothing." The monk seemed relieved. "But tomorrow night... You will take the wagon. I can give you a grulla, a little mustang, born to the desert. With them you can reach the railroad, and follow it to a town. You will have water, food... Be ready. I will come for you. At least I will not have her soul on my conscience –or yours."

He gazed intently at Fairley, as if he would force his will upon him. Fairley shrugged. He wasn't sure what to think –but he wasn't that eager to stay. "Okay."

"I will come again, this time tomorrow night. Be ready to depart. We will have to move quickly and quietly!"

He went to the door, eased it open and peered into the hall. Satisfied, he looked back at Fairley. "Till tomorrow night!" he whispered, and slipped out, locking the door again behind him. His receding footsteps made little more sound than a ghost's.

Fairley stood quietly, thinking. It had all been so strange... But his ears caught a sound in the hall. He turned his head, listening: footsteps –a shuffling gait. That had to be Juan-Bautista. Perhaps he did spy on the monk? The steps went past and faded away. Fairley waited, but heard nothing more. At length he went back to the bed, pulled off his boots, blew out the lamp and lay down.

It took him a long time to fall asleep. His mind kept going around in circles, trying to understand, to figure it out. None of it made sense –a lot of wild talk. All the same, he found himself worried about Isabella. She'd saved his life; was she really now in danger? It seemed so farfetched... Finally, he slept.

When he awoke the sun was up and the light coming through the window was already warm. He was pulling on his boots when Juan-Bautista unlocked the door and brought in his breakfast. Fairley spoke to him but got nothing but a sullen silence. When the door was closed and locked again, he looked around with a shrug. The place wasn't much different from being in jail, just more comfortable.

After eating, restless, he went to the window and looked out. The sky was brassy, the sun beating down. Nothing moved.

He stretched out on the bed again. He was still weak from his ordeal, and figured he might as well rest; he'd need his strength later if the monk meant what he said. He thought it through: if they headed south for the rail line, followed it west to the next town... No one would know him there, and they might pick up a train, get back out of the Territory. It wasn't much, but if the law thought him already dead, he might have a chance.

Some hero, he thought ruefully. Not much to pin your hopes on: no money, not even a gun, wanted by the law...

Isabella must be in a pretty bad spot if she needed help from such as him. Did she even know what the padre was planning? Would she consent to leave? He wondered...

All the padre's wild talk worried him. The full moon... the blood ritual... It sounded crazy, and Fairley hated to count on a crazy man. The whole business gave him a bad feeling.

vi.

The day went by slowly, boring and uneventful. He was looking out the window, wondering what the night would bring, when the hunchback came in with his supper. Twilight was coming on. The bell tolled, and fell silent. Fairley thought of the other monk: was he making ready even now?

As he ate, he tried to think it through again, but got nowhere. He was not a complicated man, and he'd never considered himself intelligent; in fact, he hardly thought about it. He'd lived a rough and tumble life, and when he got into trouble, he got out of it with his fists or his guns. True, even before that last job, he'd had doubts about the outlaw life, but that was just common sense. It was exciting, and when the money was good, he'd enjoyed it all, good food, girls, gambling... But usually there hadn't been any money at all, or just enough to scrape by, and most of the time he'd been on the run: covering his trail, watching his back, sleeping in the saddle or with one eye open. He'd never had a proper home nor held a decent job, and he'd never had a girl who was really his. Nor was he blind to certain other hard facts: he'd seen plenty of men killed, known of plenty more who'd been sent to prison, but he'd never known a single outlaw who retired on the wealth he'd acquired, and lived out his days in peace.

He got up again, went to the window. The moon, almost full, was rising, flooding the desert with cool, pale light. His eyes went to the cemetery with its huddle of crosses, and he thought of Xavier's story. That business with the bullet –he couldn't make that out at all. But it hardly mattered: soon the other monk would come to help him get away. Would Isabella go?

Certainly Fairley was not reluctant to leave the mission. They'd treated him kindly, but he was essentially their prisoner, and he felt sure that everything had been done for a reason. On the other hand, could he trust this other monk –Fairley didn't even know his name –or did he too have some hidden motive for his actions? Did Isabella even want to leave? In the monk's haggard look was something akin to madness, and his strange wild talk –of Lucifer, and the damnation of Isabella's soul –hardly inspired confidence.

There was a faint knocking at the door, and a key turned in the lock.

As it swung open, he expected to see the monk. Instead it was Isabella. She looked frightened. Holding a finger to her lips, she came past him into the room, and shut the door behind her.

"Señor, please forgive me," she whispered. "We hardly know each other. But I am afraid, and there is no one else to whom I can turn."

"No, no... Please," Fairley said awkwardly. The presence of this beautiful girl made him nervous and inept; what was she doing there? "If there is something I can do for you, anything, all you have to do is tell me."

"You are most kind." She moved closer to him, the scent of her perfumed hair like an intoxicant. "You will think me a foolish girl, but there is no one whom I can trust."

"But surely your uncle..."

She turned pale, her mouth tight. "My uncle, señor... is the man I fear the most." She threw her arms about him, weeping. "May God have mercy upon me!"

He led her to the chair, made her sit, and brought her a glass of water. She composed herself, smoothing her dress with both hands, and said, her voice still shaking a little: "I do not wish to seem ungrateful. My uncle has taken care of me since the death of my mother, when I was a little girl. He has been very kind... I have wanted for nothing. Everything is as it should be. But now... I sense that some awful fate is closing in upon me."

"Do you mean you're in danger?" Fairley thought of what the crazy monk had said.

"Yes, I believe so."

"And your uncle is part of what threatens you?"

"Yes."

"What kind of danger?"

"I do not know, exactly," she said. "Part of the terror is that it is unknown. I could almost face it if I knew what it was... Oh, how can I explain? It... It has something to do with his research."

Fairley thought of the 'great work'. "What is his research, exactly?"

"As if I knew! It is his greatest secret. It's some sort of scientific work, I believe... Chemistry, perhaps? He seeks something –something almost impossible to find, though again and again he has believed himself about to succeed. He and Father Alfonso work night and day."

Fairley considered this. "Chemistry? Don't know much about it... Are they making a weapon?"

"No... I don't know, perhaps; I hadn't thought of that. Whatever it is, if they find it, it will make them very powerful, and very rich."

"Men will go to great lengths for wealth," Fairley said, thinking of his own past. "But what has it got to do with you? Why do you feel threatened?"

"I sense that a crisis draws near," she said. "Danger will sometimes make itself felt. But this is more than intuition. Yesterday I overheard Father Alfonso talking to Juan-Bautista. They did not know that I could hear. Father Alfonso told the hunchback that all was almost ready. He ordered him to bring me for the ritual the night of the full moon. Señor, that is tomorrow night!" She hid her face in her hands and began to cry again.

"The ritual?" Fairley wondered out loud, recalling the other monk's words: the blood ritual. Should he tell her about him? But he saw how she suffered. He touched her gently on the arm, unsure of himself, but wanting to comfort her. "Listen... Maybe it's not... not what you think..."

She started to her feet and threw herself into his arms. "I'm afraid," she sobbed. "So afraid."

"There, there," he soothed. But she clung to him until he said, "Don't worry... I'll help you. I'll get you away from here. Nothing will happen to you. I give you my word."

Her eyes sparkled with tears. "Señor, you are most kind. But you must beware. They are very dangerous men."

"That's alright," he said, trying to muster a confidence he didn't really feel. "I can handle myself."

"You must be careful. They will kill you if they suspect you might interfere. They have killed many times before. Just this morning..."

She broke off, listening. He waited, hearing nothing. But again fear was stamped on her face.

"I must go," she said hurriedly. "I have already stayed too long. Beware! Just this morning, there was a new grave in the cemetery."

She kissed him on the cheek, listened a moment at the door, and was gone.

He sat down, exhilarated by her presence, but confused and uncertain. Her scent lingered in the air like a fading memory. He tried to make sense of what she'd told him, without really succeeding; but her fear was real enough. And who was buried in the new grave? The whole thing gave him a prickly sensation on the back of his neck.

Where was the other monk? He'd promised to be there that night. In light of what Isabella had said, his wild talk seemed less crazy. Fairley thought it through: they needed a wagon, or at least two horses, food and water for two or three days... Surely the mission had a stable, and an adequate well or spring. Food would be in the kitchen...

It grew late, and still the monk did not come. For Fairley, the wait was intolerable; they were losing their best chance. But at length he fell asleep by the window, waiting, and when he awoke, dawn was just breaking. The monk had never come.

There was still a hint of Isabella's perfume in the room. He wondered if she were safe. He'd promised to protect her! He couldn't wait any more; it was time he did something himself.

The door, to his surprise, was still unlocked. The girl hadn't locked it behind her. He cursed his foolishness –he'd wasted the whole night, waiting!

He went out and closed it softly behind him, listening. All was quiet; the mission slept. He went down the hallway like a ghost, careful to make no sound. At the courtyard he turned left under the arcade and followed it to the exterior wall. The desert air was still cool, the sun just coming up. Somewhere in the distance a coyote howled.

There, maybe fifty yards off, lay the cemetery. A new grave, the girl had said. He wondered about that... But it had to wait. He had to think about her. The crazy monk had offered him a horse. The first thing was to find it: there had to be a stable... Once he had the horse and some provisions, he'd get the girl and high-tail it out of there.

He grinned to himself: a plan like that made it all sound easy –just like robbing a bank.

He walked along the arcade, making himself think it all through. The provisions would be hardest to get, for the kitchens had to be near the monks' cells and the refectory; he'd have to watch out for the hunchback. The girl, too: he had to find her and spirit her away. It would be better to start after dark, to increase their chances in the desert, but he didn't think they could. The girl had said tonight was the night she feared –the night of the full moon...

He shook his head at that: superstitious nonsense! What was this whole business, something out of a dime novel? He was surprised that the monks, educated men, should be involved with such. But certainly the girl's fear was real.

The arcade yielded nothing but the most perfect desolation. A few tools lay in one stall, but the rest were empty, or held only some old ends of lumber or bits of dried-up harness. In places the wall had given way and he could see through to the desert beyond. At the corner he found a heavy wooden door; he shoved it open and saw the stable. Although it looked as dilapidated as everything else, it was clearly still in use. He closed the door behind him and walked to the corral.

He was in luck: no one there. He opened the gate and went into the stable. Made of adobe, like the mission, it was dark and cool, clean and well-tended. In the stalls were a big black mare, a bay, a sorrel, the grulla the monk had mentioned, a couple of burros. Something about the one horse seemed familiar, as if he'd seen it before, but he couldn't place it, and decided he was wrong. He moved among the animals, speaking softly to them and patting them, letting them get used to his scent. They seemed well cared-for, and accustomed to the desert.

This was something, anyway. Satisfied, he went back out, blinking in the hot sun. In a nearby shed was the wagon. He checked it over carefully: though old, it seemed serviceable. Next to it was a door, with a forged iron padlock hanging open on the latch. Curious, he looked inside. In a windowless room, the floor covered with straw, he found a pallet, a bucket that stank of excrement, and an iron ring fixed in the wall. The place gave him a bad feeling: it was like a prison cell... But for who?

He let himself back into the mission as quietly as he could, and paused, watchful. All was as silent as before, and he wondered about that; there was something uncanny about it.

He followed the arcade to the next corner, finding nothing. His nerves were on edge; each new mystery seemed more sinister than the last. Who had been kept prisoner in the shed? And what had happened to the crazy monk? *Was* he crazy? Fairley had seen the horse, so that much was real. Had the padre changed his mind? Or had the others discovered what he was up to? Fairley could no longer count on anyone else; that was clear. It was up to him –and tonight was the full moon. It was time to take the bull by the horns. Had he come across the girl he would have thrown caution to the wind, saddled up two horses and ridden out. But he had no idea where she was...

Now he had made almost the full circuit of the courtyard. The door to the monks' quarters was ahead. He wondered if Isabella's rooms were there, too. But something lay on the floor in front of him; he stooped and picked it up: a bit of string, with a few beads knotted along it, and a dangling little cross, carved from wood –a rosary.

He turned the broken thing over in his hand. He thought he'd seen the crazy monk with such a thing... How came it here? He tried to remember their talk in his room: his wild fears, Isabella, the grulla... Just then, something clicked in his head. An idea came to him, vague, just a suspicion, really. And he didn't like it; he didn't want it to be true. But now he had to be sure.

Through the passage, he could see again the cemetery. He made up his mind, went back to where he'd seen the tools, took a shovel and set off.

vii.

The sun was well up now, dazzling, already hot. He had little memory of the cemetery, but it was more extensive than he'd imagined. The graves, clustered along a ridge of rocky ground, spread out and away down the other side. Most were very old, maybe a couple hundred years, the names long since worn away. A few of the markers were of stone, but most were just wooden boards, leaning crazily or fallen over, shrunken and scoured bare by wind and sand.

Looking on them sobered him. Someday, he too would be dead and buried, with at most a fading marker, or maybe nothing at all. And those who still lived would be going about their lives, never knowing that he had even existed. It gave him pause –and he thought of his promise to Isabella. What mattered was what a man did here and now, while he could.

One headstone was larger and newer than the others, roughly hewn from a slab of granite, its inscription carefully but imperfectly cut. He'd had a little schooling but he couldn't make out a word of it. He guessed this was the grave of Father Xavier's master, whom he himself had buried. Fairley remembered the story the monk had told, thinking how even a man of God could come to hate. But how did he go on being a man of God?

He came to a large scattering of graves –a few dozen, perhaps, marked with rudimentary crosses, and apparently much newer. Fairley didn't like it. Hadn't Xavier said that no one had been buried here in a hundred and fifty years? So where had all these dead come from?

A few steps on, he saw the fresh grave the girl had told him of. The overturned earth was obvious, and the makeshift cross stood more or less straight and true. He walked up to it and stood looking down, doubtful and suspicious. Who was buried there? Was he right?

The sun was higher now, burning hot. He began to dig, his thoughts going round and round. He knew he couldn't figure it all out now, but his mind wouldn't stop. The problem was that none of it made any damned sense at all.

Under the brassy sky there was no sound except the chink of the shovel in the rock and sand. At least here, in the lee of the ridge, he couldn't be seen from the mission. He felt quite sure now they'd kill him if they knew what he was doing. Digging was hot, thirsty work, but the earth was sandy and dry and he went down through it quickly.

The boots appeared first –fine, expensive boots. He went more carefully after that, working around the legs, up to the waist. The dead man still wore his gunbelt, a fancy hand-tooled gunbelt that tied down around the leg. The gun was gone and so were the shells. The hands and arms emerged next. They were hard, strong hands that had done a lot of fighting, protruding stiffly now from the sleeves of a short Mexican riding jacket, its colorful embroidery soiled by the dirt of the grave. Fairley recognized that jacket. He tossed the shovel aside and reached down, grasping the dead man by the shoulders, and pulled. But the grave didn't want to give up its dead so easily. "Come on," he grunted, and gave another heave. This time the corpse pulled free and he staggered back off balance, swearing.

Gazing sightlessly up at him, the mouth twisted in a grimace and the teeth and nostrils choked with dirt, was the face of Romeo, the leader of the bandits who had robbed the train.

That settled that, anyway. He let go of the corpse and it sank back stiffly, without sound. The glassy eyes stared at him, accusing, as if to say, *I left you to die, but now I'm the one who's dead.*

Fairley shook himself. The first thing was to cover over the body again. He couldn't let them know what he'd found... He filled in the grave and tamped it down, all the time trying to think.

He didn't doubt any more; he just didn't know what it all meant. Why had the padres killed the bandit? Was he next? And the crazy monk –who clearly wasn't so crazy, after all? *'They have many dreadful ways of making a man die...'* –but to what end? And above all, the girl: what was her part in all this? Or rather, what part was destined for her? The 'blood ritual', the padre had called it.

Her life was in danger. There was no question about that. It was up to him. He'd find her and get her away from there, if it was the last thing he ever did.

The sun was high now. He headed back for the mission, the shovel against one shoulder. It felt good there, like something solid –something you could fight with. For all that, he wished he had a gun. He would have almost welcomed a confrontation. But unarmed, against three of them, the odds were a little long.

The mission was still quiet. He walked into the shaded arcade, blinded a little by the glare of the sun. Though cooler, the air was still charged with heat. He mopped his face again, and spit the dust from his mouth. Lord, he was thirsty! He had to find food and water, enough for both of them –but just now there was water in his room.

The corridor was silent and empty. Maybe the girl's room was there? He doubted it; but as he passed, he tried the doors, one after another: all locked. He opened his own door and found the room empty, just as he'd left it, the pitcher of water on the washstand. He poured a glass and drank it off, then another, feeling the water penetrate his tissues. The body dehydrated fast in this climate. He would have to be careful in the desert, especially with the girl. He thought he could take it, but she was delicate, unused to privation.

Without warning the door slammed shut behind him and a key turned in the lock. He strode to it and heard a low mocking laugh, followed by a whisper of bare feet.

Furious, he turned away without a sound. What a fool he was! The hunchback was a cagey one alright, quiet as an Indian. And Fairley had let himself get caught like a rat in a trap.

He took a deep breath, letting his anger dissipate. It only got in his way, and kept him from thinking. He pulled off his boots and stretched out on the bed. They had him where they wanted him, again. Well, that was okay: it meant they wouldn't be worrying about him. And he'd get his chance. He just hoped it wouldn't be too late.

Fairley was not a complicated man. He rolled with the punches, took things as they came; if he wanted something, he went straight for it. When his chance came, he'd grab it. But right now, there was nothing he could do. So he closed his eyes and went to sleep.

viii.

When he awoke the sun was far over in the west. He pulled on his boots and went to the window. The desert was quiet, the shadows lengthening and growing darker.

He drank some more water, going through it all again in his mind, trying to figure it; but he couldn't get anywhere. There was no way out the window. The door was too heavy and stout to force, and he had nothing with which to pick the lock. He would have to wait. He still had the shovel. He'd been docile so far, not because that was his nature –it wasn't –but he'd been waiting, feeling out the situation, trying not to make a wrong move. But now he had to act: the girl was afraid for her life, and tonight was the night everything came to a head. Just let the hunchback open the door once more and he'd have his chance...

He heard a noise in the hall, and went to the door, listening. It wasn't the hunchback's tread, but an intermittent sliding or dragging, and someone wheezing or gasping for breath. He waited, tense as a wire and hardly daring to breathe. The bell began to toll.

What now? Fairley thought. He picked up the shovel, held it in one hand. For a moment he heard nothing else. Then the key rattled in the lock, turned, and the door swung slightly inward. Fairley yanked it open. A man fell forward heavily with a groan. Fairley just caught him: it was the third monk. Fairley carried him to the bed and laid him down as gently as he could. There was blood on him and his face was pale and haggard with pain; as soon as Fairley got a good look, he knew the man was dying. He went to the door and checked the hallway: empty. The key jutted from the lock. He put it in his pocket, shut the door and went back to the bed.

The monk lay there, his breathing stertorous, his eyes almost closed. Fairley tore a strip from the bloody cassock and washed the man's face, then looked for his wounds. Great clots of blood dripped from his feet, but when Fairley touched them, the monk convulsed in pain, whimpering a little. That was when Fairley saw his hands: they were more like claws now, a sickening yellow and black, with wounds that pierced the palm. Through the backs of the hands you could see the white gleam of bone.

The monk was trying to say something. Fairley leaned close. "Forgive me, señor," he whispered. "I could not come to you last night as planned..."

"That's okay," Fairley said. "Easy... You're hurt bad."

"They discovered me," the monk went on. "The cursed hunchback... spying on me. When I went to the stable... they were waiting."

"Easy," Fairley said again, but the monk raised his palsied bloody hands.

"They crucified me," he said hoarsely. His eyes sparkled with tears. "Crucified me... Since last night I hung there, bleeding my life away. I prayed to die, I begged the Lord to let me die... He did not heed me. He knew I had one last task, before He could let me die. When I understood that... I tore myself free that I might come to you."

Fairley brought a glass of water to the monk's lips. He drank a little, and went on: "I have known Isabella all her life." He gasped for breath between the words. "I helped raise her after... after that monster destroyed her mother. He preserved the girl for the blood ritual... the most fearsome of all rites. But I will not see her life... her pure and innocent soul... thrown away, sacrificed to his ambition..."

He coughed; bloody foam came to his lips. "Now I am dying... It is up to you, señor. You must stop them."

He coughed again, a slow choking cough full of blood. His hands clutched spasmodically and his staring eyes glazed over. He was dead. Fairley straightened, looking down, full of pity and a kind of disbelief. A bit awkwardly, he crossed the dead man's hands on his breast and closed his eyes. A slow rage began to replace the sorrow in his heart. And now the bell rang again, as if tolling the monk's bitter death.

"You died because you tried to help us," he told the dead monk. "They killed you for it. And them supposed to be Christian and God-fearing men. I can't make it up to you. But I'll do my best to help Isabella, and see there's justice done them."

He felt funny saying it –him being an outlaw, a convict. But he meant it. And he knew for sure his days of robbing banks were over. Once he got out of there with her...

He took the key from his pocket and looked at it. Of antique design, the thing was heavy, made from forged iron. Fairley guessed it would unlock most of the doors in the mission.

He opened the door cautiously, found no one. He went out and locked it behind him. They had to think him still a prisoner –for if they found the dead monk, all Hell was going to break loose.

He had to find the girl –get her away from whatever devilment they were plotting. He started down the hall, trying the key in the doors. As he'd expected, it opened one after another. The first three held only dust and stale air. The fourth was furnished and fresh, and he didn't have to look in the wardrobe to know this was the girl's room, for there was just something soft and feminine about it. But she wasn't there.

"Well, damn it," Fairley muttered.

He closed the door again and moved on to the arcade. Night had fallen; there wasn't much time. The moon would be up soon –the full moon. He turned toward the church –they had to be there, where else? The dying monk' last words were going through his mind: the blood ritual... the most fearsome of rites... her innocent soul sacrificed...

The silence of the mission was complete. Though he walked like a cat, his footsteps seemed to ring along the arcade. If only he had a gun! Counting the hunchback, there were three of them, and he only had the shovel –and his fists. He had never backed down from a fight –he'd stand up to any man –but the odds were against him and he'd have to be careful.

He passed into the refectory, found no one, and on into the kitchen –they'd need food before they left –and came to a narrow corridor with doors at regular intervals, probably the cells of the monks. He hesitated, wondering if he might find a weapon there –and at that moment he heard, muffled and far away, a woman scream.

The sound was cut off suddenly, as if stifled. Unsure where it had come from, Fairley hurried to the door at the end and found himself in a sort of vestibule. Heavy robes, musty and ragged, hung on hooks along one wall, and on a table lay a large Bible, closed with iron hasps. To the left was a door: that had to be the church. Fairley eased it open and went through.

To his surprise he found no one. The broad high space was cool and shadowy, the air hushed, smelling of dust and stale incense. He walked to the center of the nave, peering about as his eyes adjusted. The church was built in the shape of a cross, the walls covered with obscure frescoes, and before him rose the altar, tall and massive, carved from dark wood. Near the door where he'd entered a tallow candle burned, without which the place would have been pitch-black. The pews were jumbled together, and covered with dust and cobwebs. Clearly, there'd been no services in a long time.

Baffled, he turned to the entrance door. Its heavy mesquite wood, black with age, was barred on the inside. To one side, a dark aperture led to a spiral staircase, doubtless mounting to the bell-tower. Fairley turned back, frustrated, his nerves on edge. He couldn't understand it: where were they? Where had that scream come from? None of it made any sense. Was there some hidden or secret room?

He moved down the far wall, finding nothing, but as he passed behind the altar, he heard a brief sound, like a door opening and closing, and the murmur of a voice. He froze. From his left came the sound of shuffling steps, and he saw, pushing open a trap door in the floor, the twisted form of Juan-Bautista.

ix.

So there was a crypt *below* the church! –but without stopping to think, Fairley dropped the shovel and threw himself on the hunchback. Taken by surprise, Juan-Bautista went down, but Fairley couldn't hold him. Snarling, the hunchback wriggled free and turned on him, lashing out. Fairley took a one-two punch in the face, then closed with the little man, smashing a fist into his belly, another to his jaw. The hunchback shook them off, growling; he bowed his head and drove in, butting Fairley in the stomach. Fairley fell back and down, and the hunchback leapt on him, swinging hard. Fairley couldn't believe the crippled man was so strong. He took two pounding blows to the head, jarring him, and felt fingers at his throat. Kneeing upward to shove the hunchback off, he stumbled to his feet. But now Juan-Bautista pulled a long knife from his belt.

They circled warily, Fairley watching the blade. The shovel was out of reach. The hunchback lunged forward, slashing viciously left then right. Fairley dodged, chopped down across the hunchback's wrist, and punched him in the face, left-right. Blood pouring from his nose, Juan-Bautista muttered something and came on again, swinging the knife back and forth. Fairley wasn't quick enough, and the blade cut hard across his left arm, burning like hot steel. Pain goading him on, he slammed his fists into the hunchback's ribs, felt bones break. Juan-Bautista gasped but swung the knife again. As he stepped back, Fairley's foot banged against the shovel. He grabbed it up and swung. The flat of the blade hit Juan-Bautista's skull, and he fell to the floor and lay still.

Breathing hard, Fairley turned him over. The little man looked bad, but he was still alive. Fairley knew he should kill him, but he didn't have the heart. His arm throbbed, the blood flowing steadily. He tore a strip from the hunchback's shirt and bound it around the wound. He was shaken and battered from the fight, but there was no time to lose. The girl was in danger. He picked up the knife, wiped it off, and went to the trapdoor.

From it descended a steep spiral staircase, formed from rough-hewn stone. Fairley went down it blindly, by feel, trying to make as little noise as possible. It was like descending into a pit. He felt the hairs rise on the back of his neck in spite of himself. This hidden crypt was more fitting for the dead than the living, and in his nose was a charnel scent of dry bones turned to dust.

At the bottom stood a half-open wooden door; beyond, there was light, and a murmur of sound. He crept to it, wondering. Was this the 'great work' which Father Xavier had vaunted? —or the place of frightful death and perdition of the soul that the dead monk had warned him of? Either way, demons or devils, you're getting Isabella out of there, he told himself. Her life depends on you.

He eased open the door, peering into the crypt. Nearest to him, the place resembled some sort of laboratory. Jars were ranged on shelves like in an apothecary's shop; and on a long table, pitted and burnt, was a strange collection of apparatus for chemical experiments: crucibles, retorts, long-spouted beakers, grills and braziers, and a sort of oven or furnace. To one side were evil-looking wooden devices and machines, with leather straps for restraints; and at the end was what looked like an altar, lit with candles, before which stood the two monks.

"The time draws near, Xavier." He recognized Alfonso's voice.

"Indeed," the other answered. "We must take the final steps."

"This one will please the Master!" Alfonso spoke eagerly. "This time we shall not fail!"

"Oh?" Fairley could see Xavier's face, disdainful and aloof, as he glanced at the other monk. "It is true that, till now, we have been hindered by impure souls. Such crimes have not won the Master's favor. It must be otherwise tonight."

"It will!" Alfonso urged. "She is still a virgin... What more could we do to satisfy him?"

They were talking about Isabella! A grim resolve settled itself within Fairley. Whatever they were planning... But where was she? He'd heard her scream...

"We shall see... I warn you, Alfonso: most of the ancient texts concur. Without the aid of Lucifer himself, the Philosopher's Stone will not be discovered. But to invoke Satan, no crime will suffice, not even the blood ritual and the black mass. To succeed, to finally reach our goal, so long sought, so much desired, we must needs alienate our existences, renounce of salvation –and abandon our souls to him."

"No!" Alfonso said. "I will not! Anything but that."

"You are a coward, Alfonso," Xavier said. "By your lack of courage, you foredoom yourself to failure. But not I! The whole world holds not another such as I! My ambition knows no limits. And I will dare all –dare *all*, to win all."

Alfonso laughed. "You are ever the same, Xavier –your pale boasts, and vague imprecations. But I am no child, to be intimidated by your posturing and your empty threats. You, what have you done? You trifle with your powders and potions, while I plunge my hands into the still-warm entrails of my victims. Go to the cemetery and count their graves! I have sinned –royally, magnificently. No, I shall not give up my soul. You are wrong. My crimes shall suffice, for they might equal those of Lucifer himself!"

"You fool," Xavier said. Fairley could see his face –a mask of scorn. "By your vainglory and your cowardice, you risk everything! You, rival Lucifer! Ha! You are less than a worm that crawls in the earth, less than a maggot that writhes in a rotting corpse, beside the Master."

"Mind how you speak to me, Xavier," Alfonso warned angrily. "You go too far."

"Do I, Alfonso? Do I go... *too far?*"

Shocked by what he'd heard, Fairley watched in disbelief as Father Xavier took a heavy candlestick and, turning without warning, clubbed Alfonso in the back of the skull. The stricken monk gasped; he sank to his knees, groaning. Xavier dragged him to the altar and raised him up, holding his chin so it exposed the neck. In his right hand he brandished a serpentine dagger. "In nomine Luciferi!" he cried, and slashed the knife across Alfonso's throat. The blood splattered the altar, and Alfonso went limp. Xavier dropped the corpse and stood over it, still gripping the gory blade.

"Weakling!" he hissed between clenched teeth, eyes glittering madly. "Coward! You thought to save your unclean soul! But without absolution, it goes straight to Hell. Vaunt your crimes now! Tell Satan how you rival him!"

But seeming to recall his true purpose, he turned away. "Bah!" he muttered. "I trifle with worms while the great work waits before me, and time is short." He took a heavy watch from his cassock. "Midnight soon. Where is that lout, Juan-Bautista?" He glared about.

Fairley drew back, as a cold finger of fear touched him. He was no coward: he'd faced marshals, posses, Indians and desperadoes, but the monk seemed beyond the ken of ordinary men, almost superhuman. He might be capable of anything.

Xavier went again to his task. Lighting a candle before him, he opened a great leather-bound book and began to intone some sort of incantation. Fairley couldn't make out a word but its very sound was baleful. He shook himself. He had to do something —find the girl and get her out of this madhouse! But how? Where was she?

He slipped forward, trying to make out what the monk was doing; and that was when he saw her. She lay on the velvet-covered altar, stretched at full length, and wrapped carelessly in a black cloak. One arm and her legs, naked to the thighs, were spattered with the dead monk's blood. Her head was turned to one side and he could not see her face, just the mass of black hair; but he could tell that she still breathed, though slowly, as if she slept. Drugged, Fairley thought. At least she was still alive. The bloody dagger lay beside her, next to a smoldering burner.

If only he had a gun! Surprise was on his side, but the monk was bigger and more powerful, with the dagger ready to hand. Fairley had only the hunchback's knife, and he glanced around, looking for something, anything he might use as a weapon. But there was only the strange chemical apparatus, flimsy, and ineffective. Why hadn't he brought the shovel?

The monk droned on, reading from the great book, his voice rising now, louder and more imperious. The candles dimmed for a moment, all at once, then flamed up again, brighter than before. Xavier took a handful of incense, and with a curious gesture, he threw it on the burner. Smoke boiled out, and an awful reek filled the crypt. Now –Fairley couldn't believe his eyes –*something* took form in the smoke, a shape like a face, huge and terrible.

Xavier drew himself up to his full height. His voice rang out the words of the incantation –and now the shape spoke *with him* in a voice like thunder. The monk tossed aside the folds of the cloak that covered the girl, and she lay nude on the altar. Her head turned from side to side, as if she said no, and her lips moved a little. Fairley saw a strange design like a five-pointed star painted in scarlet on the pale skin of her belly. As the shape in the smoke laughed, gloating, the monk seized the dagger and raised it over his head.

Fairley felt a rush of anger, cold and purposeful. He'd put a stop to this, if he had to kill Xavier with his bare hands. He pulled the hunchback's knife from his belt and rose, trying not to look at the thing in the smoke that froze the blood in his veins. But *it saw him*, and roared forth some warning. Xavier turned, rage twisting his face. "Fool!" he spat. "Dare you profane the invocation of the Master, Lucifer himself?" But he threw back his head and laughed. Behind, the thing in the smoke laughed with him.

"Come ahead, Señor Fairley," the monk said. "Come and meet your death. It will give me pleasure."

Grimly, Fairley started toward him –and then someone shoved him from behind, knocking him sideways and down. The knife flew from his hand and some of the apparatus crashed to the floor. As he tried to get to his feet, hands grabbed his head and slammed it against the table. Black spots boiled before his eyes, the pain nauseating. He shoved back blindly and shook his head, trying to clear it. There before him, battered and soaked in his own blood, was Juan-Bautista. The hunchback was swaying a little, unsteady on his feet, but there was hate and bloodlust on his face. His lips snarled back from rotting teeth, and he hurled himself forward, hands clawing for Fairley's eyes. Fairley staggered back against the table, put a boot in the hunchback's chest and shoved hard. Juan-Bautista crashed back against the shelves, knocking some of the jars to the floor.

Now the shape in the smoke was roaring in rage. The monk shouted, his face a mask of fury, as he pointed to Fairley with the dagger. Behind him, the girl stirred a little, groggily. The hunchback seized a jar and hurled it. Fairley ducked, but liquid spattered him, caustic and burning like acid. Juan-Bautista reached for another. Fairley grabbed him and spun him around. He brushed aside a punch, hammered the hunchback's head with his fists, and smashed a right into his broken nose. Juan-Bautista reeled back, moaning in pain. Fairley grabbed him, picked him up and threw him bodily against the wall. Bottles and jars crashed down from falling shelves. The hunchback lay where he fell.

Out of breath, his skin seared by the acid, Fairley turned to face the monk. What he saw was barely human.

Xavier's eyes burned with unholy fire, madness writhing across his face. He drew himself up, the dagger in one outflung hand. Behind him, the shape in the smoke twisted and convulsed in fury, its voice, like a great tree cracking and breaking asunder, calling down imprecations.

"Fool!" the monk roared. "You cannot stop the blood ritual! Did you think to save the girl? –but she is mine to do with as I will: my daughter! My own sister bore her to me. And tonight her destiny is fulfilled! I shall carve Lucifer's name in her naked flesh –stain the black altar of sacrifice with her virgin blood!"

He turned to face the shape and raised the dagger over the girl. "In nomine..."

Fairley charged forward and chopped him in the back of the neck with both hands. The monk toppled off balance, knocking over the candles, but he turned as quickly as a cat, and slashed viciously with the dagger. The blade tore through Fairley's shirt and cut him across the chest. Ignoring the pain, he blocked a second slash and drove his fist into the monk's belly. Xavier only grunted and jabbed the blade at his throat. Fairley dodged it but slipped on the floor, slick with blood. Growling, Xavier gripped the dagger with both hands and drove it down; Fairley rolled aside, the knife barely missing him. He kicked the monk behind the knee and scrambled to his feet, hands outstretched, shifting his weight from side to side. The monk came for him, slashing back and forth. Fairley tried to block the dagger but it caught his wounded arm and he grunted in pain. Xavier laughed and swung the knife again.

Desperate now, Fairley dodged the blade and drove forward, head down, butting Xavier in the chest. Caught by surprise, the monk stumbled. He lost his footing, and fell back, his skull slamming against the altar. Fairley stepped up and punched him in the head, left-right-left. The dazed monk stabbed wildly with the knife, but Fairley knocked it away. He smashed a right to Xavier's jaw and felt something break. The monk's eyes rolled up; he sank back. The shape in the smoke was screaming like a banshee.

Coughing and out of breath, Fairley realized the crypt was full of flames. He looked around: the spilled chemicals had caught fire, and now the whole place was burning: wooden tables, torture machines, the velvet of the altar...

He turned to it, coughing, eyes burning. As he reached for Isabella, she opened her eyes, confused and afraid. He wrapped her in the black cloak and picked her up. She clung to him, trembling.

"It's okay, señorita," he said. "We're getting out of here."

The full moon was still high when he drew up the wagon on the ridge and looked back. The old timbers, furniture, even the adobe, were all bone-dry; the mission burned like a torch. Even as they watched, the roof of the church collapsed with a crash, sending a shower of sparks into the air. Fire was purifying the Mission of Our Lady of Sorrows.

Isabella was still trembling, and Fairley saw tears in her eyes. He didn't say anything, just put his arm around her and turned the wagon toward the south.